WITHDRAWN W9-ABY-259

WITHDRAWN

Erec

PT
1534
.E8
1982

EREC
by
HARTMANN VON AUE

TRANSLATED, WITH AN INTRODUCTION,
BY J. W. Thomas

UNIVERSITY OF NEBRASKA PRESS
LINCOLN AND LONDON

Salem Academy and College
Gramley Library
Winston-Salem, N.C. 27108

The paper in this book meets the guidelines for permanence and durability of the Committee on Production Guidelines for Book Longevity of the Council on Library Resources.

Publishers on the Plains

UNP

Copyright © 1982 by the University of Nebraska Press
All rights reserved
Manufactured in the United States of America

Library of Congress Cataloging in Publication Data
Hartmann, von Aue, 12th cent.
  Erec.

  I. Thomas J. W. (John Wesley), 1916– II. Title.
PT1534.E8   1982   831'.2   81–7471
ISBN 0–8032–4408–8

CONTENTS

PREFACE

As the earliest Arthurian verse-novel in the German language, Hartmann von Aue's *Erec* was highly influential, not only on the many Arthurian works that followed, but also on courtly narrative verse in general. However, his tale is of more than antiquarian interest. Its subjects—the individual in conflict with society and the destructive force of possessive love— are modern, and its language, when transferred into prose, is more direct and lucid than most contemporary writing. Indeed, it was the conviction that the story deserved a much larger audience than that of medieval scholars which inspired this translation, the first into English.

The preparation of the introduction to the translation was greatly facilitated by the assistance of the Interlibrary Loan Department of the University of Kentucky Library and by a grant from the University Research Committee which supported my study in other libraries.

INTRODUCTION

Hartmann's Life and Works

"There was a knight so learned that he read from books whatever he found written in them; his name was Hartmann, and he was a servant at Aue." With these opening lines to his novella *Der arme Heinrich* (Poor Henry) the author introduces himself and supplies all of the certain knowledge we have of the life of medieval Germany's most influential writer. Additional, but less reliable, biographical data can be gleaned from further personal comments in his works, dialectal peculiarities of his language, brief comments about him by other poets of the time, and a fourteenth-century illumination that ascribes to him an identifiable coat of arms. Together they suggest that Hartmann lived in the northern part of the present-day canton of Zurich (possibly in the Rhine town of Eglisau or on the island of Reichenau), composed between 1180 and 1203, went on a crusade, and died sometime after 1210 and before 1220.

Assuming a steady development in his facility of expression and independence of thought, the relative chronology of Hartmann's five major works and his sixteen songs is fairly clear. The earliest was *Die Klage* (The Lament), a poem of nearly two thousand verses which propounds the conventional doctrine of courtly love in an argument between the heart and the body. Next came the courtly love songs, traditional compositions that display more technical proficiency than depth of feeling. They were followed by *Erec* and then by *Gregorius*, a church legend in the form of a courtly novel, whose theme is that a man can forsake the role which God has ordained for him only at the risk

1

of ruining his life and losing his soul. After the two novels a
second group of songs appeared, superior to the first ones, which
forgo the service of the highborn lady, renounce secular and
temporal values, and advocate the love and service of God.
Stylistically the most mature and presumably the latest works
are *Der arme Heinrich* and *Iwein*. The first is a medieval version
of the Job story in which the hero initially fails God's testing; the
other is an Arthurian novel that exposes the selfishness of the
Arthurian emphasis on worldly honor and contrasts it with the
ideal of true kindness. These writings show a greater variety
than those of any other German poet of the period, and each of
the longer works except *Iwein* was the first of its kind in German
literature.

Hartmann composed at a time when German works were
more strongly influenced than ever before or since by French
writings. The latter made up a sophisticated, courtly literature
that dealt largely in superficial conceits and stressed artistry,
wit, and imagination to the almost complete exclusion of real
life. Like most other German poets of his day, Hartmann drew
largely from this source for his subject matter, and at first also
displayed the prevailing French attitude toward literature.
However, he was both a practical man and a moralist, one whose
nature was basically antagonistic toward the concept of art as
escapism or mere entertainment. After an apprenticeship of
imitation, with *Die Klage* and the courtly love songs, he began to
place his own characteristic stamp on his material. *Erec* marks
the turning point.

Theme

When Hartmann composed his *Erec* (ca. 1190), he introduced
medieval Germany to a type of fiction, the Arthurian verse-
novel, which was to remain popular for the next three hundred
years. A skillfully written work, *Erec* not only created a taste for
similar narratives but also established norms of style, structure, content, and language that lasted until the beginning of
the modern period. Like the Welsh *Gereint* and the Norse *Erex
Saga*, Hartmann's story is based primarily on the *Erec et Enide*

of Chrétien de Troyes, whose general plot it used while changing details and the underlying idea.[1] It is considerably longer than the French romance. Except for four rather short fragments, *Erec* survived only in a single, late manuscript, minus its introduction and with several other lacunae. Fortunately, however, the fragments—three of which are from the first half of the thirteenth century—attest to the general reliability of the chief manuscript and fill one of the longer hiatuses. With regard to the particular setting, the lost beginning—variously estimated at 77 to about 150 lines—can be replaced from Chrétien's version, but what Hartmann may have said there concerning his specific theme must be deduced from the story itself.[2]

The plot of *Erec* turns about the conflict between happiness in the framework of aristocratic society, what is called the joy of the court, and private pleasure which estranges the individual from society. The joy of the court was based on great celebrations with feasting, dancing, and professional entertainers; large, formal hunting parties; and especially the colorful tournaments in which the knight did homage to the aristocratic community by striving for its praise and the latter honored him and itself by applauding him. This collective happiness not only provided the esprit de corps that ensured domestic peace and tranquillity, but also established a reputation abroad that attracted valiant knights and facilitated alliances to defend the land from foreign powers. The particular private pleasure that threatened the joy of the court was possessive, sexual love, examples of which are introduced in constant succession throughout the work.[3]

In the missing beginning Gawein warns King Arthur against observing the tradition of the hunt of the white stag, according to which the one who kills the stag is to kiss the most beautiful woman at the court, because he fears that the love and loyalty of the knights for their ladies will jeopardize the harmony and solidarity of their community. Fortunately, a confrontation is postponed and later avoided, partly as a result of a second conflict between society and possessive love which unexpectedly occurs on the day of the hunt.

Queen Guinevere, a maid in waiting, and the youthful Erec are following the hunters at a distance when Iders, his beautiful lady, and a dwarf attendant ride past. The queen sends the maiden and then Erec to find out who the knight and lady are, but they are driven away by the dwarf, who strikes them viciously with a whip. At the time, Iders's conduct in allowing this is inexplicable, but later, after we have observed the antisocial and brutal actions of Mabonagrin, the cause of the knight's behavior becomes obvious: he is protecting his closed society of two against the threat of being merged into the larger community of nobility. The offense to Guinevere is symbolic, for she, even more than Arthur, represents the unifying force of the court.

Knight, lady, and dwarf, followed at a distance by Erec, then journey on to Tulmein Castle, where Iders again endangers the joy of the court by threatening to seize for his lady by force a prize intended for the winner of a beauty contest. By now it is clear that he is motivated by something other than mere arrogance, indeed that he is driven by an excessive devotion to his loved one which cannot tolerate the idea that another could be more beautiful. In the ensuing battle he is defeated by Erec and sent back to Guinevere. Here he is freed of his obsession by admitting that his lady is not the most beautiful of women, and the two are integrated into the queen's retinue. Thus, with an irony typical of Hartmann, we see that the dwarf's blows bring about the very end they were intended to forestall.

The conflict between the individual and society begins to involve the hero and heroine even before Gawein's fears are allayed and Iders and his lady pass out of the story. The first hint of this appears in an unexpected and somewhat insolent statement by Erec that at once reminds us of his opponent. On the morning of the conflict at Tulmein the youth refuses Duke Imain's offer of better clothing for Enite, saying that he will show the knights and ladies that his sword could ensure her high praise if she were bare as his hand and blacker than coal. After such a remark, the loving glances that hero and heroine exchange on the way to Arthur's court seem noteworthy, and their later torment at having to wait to satisfy their sexual desires appears ominous. To be sure, Erec's success and resultant fame at the tournament show no trace of alienation from the joy of the court, although Hartmann's audience might have been warned of trouble ahead by the praise the youth receives from the admiring spectators. When he is compared to Solomon in wisdom, Absalom in beauty, Sampson in strength, and Alexander in generosity, the medieval audience might have remembered the tales in which all four of these worthies were betrayed or brought to shame because of love for a woman. In any event, we are not greatly surprised later when Erec and Enite so neglect the joy of their own court that the courtly society falls into decay and knights desert it.[4]

Hartmann's theme reappears briefly with the account of the two robbers who renounce other booty in order to claim Enite—thus showing that lust can be a stronger threat to society than greed—and in greater detail in the story of the unnamed count which follows. He had been a decent man of honor until love's snare taught him treachery. His attempt to take Enite by force not only violates the integrity of society in general—since established custom requires him to respect the rights of guests in his land—but also changes the joy of his own court to the shame of defeat and to grief at the death of six of its knights.

Quite different perspectives on the joy of the court are supplied by the next two episodes. The reference to it in the first meeting with Guivreiz is short, but significant. When the squires of the small king run forth from the castle gate, they are jubilant because they think he has conquered Erec. However, there is no indication that Guivreiz's retinue is saddened to learn of his defeat. The happiness of courtly society apparently does not necessarily depend on success at arms. It depends on solidarity, as is shown by Erec's chance encounter with King Arthur's court.

In some ways the meeting resembles that between the Arthurian society and Iders. Once again the community reaches out to the individual through two representatives, on this occasion Keii and Gawein. The former gets a blow for his pains, as did Guinevere's first messenger, and the latter a scolding. Still, Erec, unlike Iders, is not intent on defending his private happiness and closed society against a larger community, but rather on putting his personal affairs in order so that he can feel comfortable in one. "Who comes to court as little suited for courtly life as I am now would be better off at home," he says. "A man should be happy at court and behave accordingly. I cannot do that now and must abstain from courtly activity like one disabled." Even this temporary defection of a former member dims the court's joy for a time, and its festive hunt comes to an abrupt end.

The following adventure presents a marked contrast to the confrontation between the Arthurian community and Iders, for, where the latter used the rude violence of the dwarf to keep society at a distance, Cadoc was prevented by the violence of lawless giants from joining society. Erec, although still an exile from the joy of the court, praises it to the knight and sends him and his lady to Guinevere to represent him in her retinue. The actions of both the dwarf and the giants show how easily cruelty can take possession of those who live outside the conventions of organized society.

The perfect object lesson with respect to Hartmann's theme is provided by Count Oringles. Although he knows that proper behavior is necessary to preserve the tranquillity and reputation of his court, he is so overcome by his passion for Enite that he deliberately offends both his guests and his retinue: first by the hasty marriage to an unwilling bride, then by beating her in their presence. His sudden, unheroic death appears as a well-deserved punishment, while the demise of the joy of his court is strikingly portrayed in the mass flight from the castle. At the same time, in marked contrast to the social disintegration taking place, Erec and Enite, who have traveled as isolated individuals since leaving Karnant, prepare to rebuild their own society by forming a community of two.

This community quickly grows with the addition of Guivreiz and his men, and the hero and heroine never again journey alone. Their stay at Guivreiz's castle gives us a description of an ideal environment for hunting, one of the chief courtly pleasures, and also represents the final step in their reintegration into society. Erec has recovered in spirit as well as in body when he moves on to the Brandigan adventure, which provides a final example, better documented than the others, of the struggle between the joy of the court and a possessive, alienating love. Unconsciously serving as an agent of society, Erec here frees a knight who has bitterly defended a prison which possessive love built for him. With regard to the joy of the court, the episode ends quite differently than that at Limors as a rejuvenated society welcomes back its exiles with a four-week celebration.[5] When he returns to Arthur's court, Erec is highly honored by the knights for his brave deeds, while the wise king praises him for greatly increasing the splendor (and joy) of his court by adding eighty beautiful ladies to it. The hero and heroine soon journey on to Karnant. Since the reconciliation at Limors, their company has grown steadily—which is thematically significant—and they enter the city with six thousand nobles. Erec began his reign well, with festive hospitality, says the narrator, ruled the land so that it was at peace, and governed his devotion to Enite by propriety. They had learned to subordinate their private pleasures to the joy of the court.

Throughout the work the possessive love that threatens society is symbolized, naturally enough, by feminine beauty, which is mentioned frequently. The story begins with two successive beauty contests and a reference to the loveliness of Iders's companion. The narrator introduces Enite by saying that she was the most beautiful maiden of whom he had ever heard and stresses the sensual nature of her beauty by praising the swan-white body that gleamed through the tears in her clothing. Many subsequent scenes open with a comment on her lovely appearance. The cultured members of the Round Table are so startled by it that they stare openly, and none think of objecting when Arthur proclaims her the prettiest lady at the court. King Lac finds her beauty a feast for the eyes, and the robber lookout, the squire, the unnamed count, Guivreiz, Oringles, and the townspeople at Brandigan declare her to be the most beautiful woman they have ever seen.

In the Mabonagrin episode the beauty motif shifts to this knight's lady, who is lovelier than any woman but Enite, and to the eighty widows, not included in Chrétien's story, whose beauty is described at length. The account of Mabonagrin's companion illustrates the danger of feminine beauty, for she deliberately tricked her lover into abandoning society, and it also explains Erec's earlier suspicions concerning Enite. The subsequent history of the widows, on the other hand, shows that woman's beauty can greatly enhance the joy of the court and thus support society. Still, it becomes evident during the fearful battle in the park that the power of beauty cannot match that of loyal devotion. Mabonagrin, who loses, had been strengthened by the sight of his lady's beauty, while Erec, the victor, had been sustained by the thought of Enite's love, a self-sacrificing affection that is much more than sexual passion.

Since the Arthurian court is used repeatedly as an example of a joyous and harmonious society, the probable source of Hartmann's theme is particularly interesting. During the opening scene of Chrétien's *Yvain,* Arthur's knights are astonished and greatly annoyed to see their king leave them in the midst of a large festival to go to his chamber and make love with the queen. There are several strong indications that the German author knew *Yvain* when he began *Erec.*

Plot Structure and the Development of the Hero

Like many medieval narratives, *Erec* presents its theme and tells its story largely by means of parallel actions, which produce a more or less symmetrical framework. It has a dual structure that consists simultaneously of two parts and five parts. The two-part system divides Erec's experiences into a first and second chain of events, each of which tells of the fall and rise of the hero's fortunes from shame and disgrace through trials and conflicts to honor and kingship. The first series ends with the arrival of the newly wedded couple in Karnant and serves as an introduction to the second, which is longer and of much greater significance. The five-part system groups the episodes as follows: (1) Iders, Arthur's court, Karnant; (2) the robbers, the unnamed count, Guivreiz; (3) Arthur's court: Keii, Gawein, the court; (4) the giants, Count Oringles, Guivreiz; (5) Mabonagrin, Arthur's court, Karnant. The events of section one parallel those of section five, and the events of section two parallel those of section four, thus suggesting comparisons that illuminate the conflict between the joy of the court and possessive love and also trace the development of the hero. The fact that each section consists of three episodes with three different locales probably has no thematic significance and only reflects the medieval interest in form.[6]

Important departures from Chrétien's text at both ends indicate that Hartmann's basic plan was quite different from that of his source. The French poet begins with a hero who at twenty-five is already famous and takes him only to the point when he is about to return home a second time as king. Hartmann starts with a younger, impulsive, and quite inexperienced Erec, stresses his development, and concludes with an account of his successful reign. His work is clearly an education novel in which the hero learns through varied experiences what one needs to know and be in order to rule a country well.[7]

The episodes of sections one and five present events in a rising scale of importance that reflect the increasing fame of the hero. The similarity of the corresponding scenes emphasizes the difference in Erec's behavior as a youth and as a mature man and thereby shows his progress. The story of both sections can be summarized thus:

Against the urgent advice of a royal companion, the hero resolves to challenge a renowned and greatly feared warrior. He rides into a region which is unknown to him, through a town that is celebrating a festival, and to a castle beyond, where he inquires about his opponent and spends the night. In the morning he attends mass and then goes to the grounds where the conflict is to take place. During the long struggle he is inspired to great valor by Enite and is finally victorious. He spares the life of his opponent although the latter threatened to kill him. The defeated knight and his beautiful lady are received into courtly society, while the ruler of the land and his subjects jubilantly celebrate Erec's triumph. The hero feels compassion for some people there who have suffered great misfortune, resolves to improve their lot, and later—with the help of King Arthur—manages to do so.

Erec now rides to Arthur's realm, bringing with him (in one) a strikingly beautiful maiden or (in five) eighty beautiful ladies, who come not properly dressed for the court. New clothing is supplied, and the court is pleased and enhanced. The hero receives high honors and shows his generosity. At last he and Enite depart for Karnant, where they are welcomed enthusiastically and made king and queen of the land.

A comparison of the scene in which the youthful Erec laments his humiliation and begs Guinevere to let him pursue Iders with the later one in which the hero confidently rebuts Guivreiz's warnings about the more famous Mabonagrin clearly shows the progress he has made. It is also possible that the motive behind his decision to challenge the second knight indicates an increased maturity. The hero's reasons for wanting to fight Iders were completely personal—he almost forgot the attack on Guinevere's maid in waiting and the insult to the queen—but his reasons for fighting Mabonagrin may be largely political. Knowing that he had lost the respect of his subjects when they began to doubt his manhood, he wishes to seize the opportunity to settle that question forever and thus strengthen his future reign.

On the morning of the battle with Iders, Erec went to mass and then ate breakfast, both as a matter of course. However, before he fights Mabonagrin he not only attends mass, but prays very earnestly that God will preserve his life, drinks St. John's blessing, and is careful to eat only a little: the narrator commends him for being properly concerned. During the conflict with Iders, Erec was strengthened by the sight of Enite's beauty, which later betrayed him, while it is the thought of her love that sustains him during the Mabonagrin struggle. His courteous treatment of Mabonagrin afterwards compares most favorably with Erec's petty ridicule of the defeated Iders.[8]

The improved behavior of the hero is made apparent by his interaction with two opponents whose characters and situations are very similar. Each of them avoids society, maintains his isolation by violence, and is devoted to a beautiful lady. After they are conquered, Iders confesses his error to Guinevere, Mabonagrin explains his situation to Erec, and both they and their ladies rejoin courtly society. A hint that Iders, like Mabonagrin, had been tricked into antisocial behavior by his lady is contained in his assertion to the queen that he, like the hare caught in the net, had been wary at the wrong time.

Before returning to Arthur's court after the Iders adventure, Erec shows his sympathy for Enite's impoverished parents by promising to make them rich. When he later does so, with the help of King Arthur and King Lac, he demonstrates a commendable, although certainly not disinterested, compassion. On the other hand, the parallel situation at Brandigan, where he becomes concerned with the grief of eighty widows and takes them along to Arthur's court so that they might have a happier life, reveals the impersonal compassion of a benevolent monarch. Moreover, in the second instance, many more people are affected.

The ladies have been at his court only a short time when Arthur prevails on them to cease grieving and turn their lives to joy, whereupon he gives them dresses of silver and gold to replace their black garments. This transformation may throw some light on the earlier and comparable episode involving Enite. When she arrived at Arthur's court in section one, she was still wearing tattered clothing, for Erec had twice refused the offer of her wealthy uncle to dress her better. Guinevere at once decked her out in the finest garments. Since Hartmann's narrator, unlike Chrétien's, does not tell us why Erec rejected Duke Imain's proposal, one might think that he wanted to prove at Arthur's court what he had maintained at Tulmein Castle, that "one should decide on the basis of her person, not her dress, whether or not a woman is beautiful." However, the case of the widows indicates that the clothing of Enite was a matter of ritual and symbolism. They renounce grief to be inducted into the joy of the court and are therefore appropriately arrayed. Enite is to become a queen and therefore should make her initial formal appearance before the Round Table in the attire of a queen.[9]

With regard to fame as a knight, the first and last returns of Erec to Arthur's court present a strong contrast. When he came back from the Iders episode, he was a youth who had won his first combat and was eager to earn praise and renown. In the tournament that followed he jousted early and late and once even rode into the fray without his helmet. No tournament is held during his final appearance at the court since there is no need for the hero to prove himself. The narrator briefly comments that Erec received the crown of honor and was praised as being unmatched for bravery and because no one in all the lands had succeeded in such great adventures. A similar revelation with regard to Erec's development is seen in the manifestation of his generosity on the two occasions. After the tournament he

Salem Academy and College
Gramley Library
Winston-Salem, N.C. 27108

was praised for his liberality because he had collected no booty from knights and had given away several horses to mercenaries. When he leaves Arthur's court the last time his charity is more thoughtful: "he gave as much as he could to the poor, who could use his wealth, each according to his need."

The arrangement of events in parallel is, of course, most effective with the two episodes in Karnant, the scene of Erec's greatest failure and greatest success. On both occasions Erec and Enite leave Arthur's court with an imposing escort and are met on the way by a large delegation which had traveled three days to meet them. In keeping with the principle of a rising scale, the second reception is much larger and more elaborate, but the situations are kept sufficiently similar to accentuate Erec's exemplary conduct as he begins his second reign. Where he formerly had neglected the joy of the court for private pleasure, he now arranges the most splendid festival the land has ever known and thereafter rules himself and his country wisely.

The correspondence of the events of sections two and four is even closer than that of one and five and is equally revealing. Although the time difference is small—there is no contrast between youth and maturity—the difference in the hero's attitude is pronounced, which evokes comparisons that reveal his progress. A distinctive aspect of these two series of adventures is that Enite plays as prominent a role as does Erec. In both of them hero and heroine set out on a random journey. They first encounter outlaws, whom Erec kills, and then a count who falls in love with Enite and determines to have her as a wife. Erec strikes him down, and he and Enite flee from the wrath of the count's subjects. Soon afterwards they meet Guivreiz, whom Erec fights with mixed results before the three go off together to the little king's castle.

Erec's opponents present an ascending scale not only with regard to rank—low, middle, and high—but also with respect to social morality: the enemies of the established mores, the knight who accepts them but fails to observe them, and the exemplary nobleman. In section two, Erec's mood is one of bitter alienation, which decreases toward the end. This improvement is seen in his sparing the life of Guivreiz and ceasing to threaten Enite. Section four portrays three stages in the hero's rehabilitation: concern for others, reconciliation with Enite, and reintegration into society.[10] When Erec was waylaid by the robbers at the beginning of the earlier journey, he made a most uncourtly impression. He killed all of them, although it is likely that some tried to flee; roughly berated Enite for warning him and possibly saving his life; burdened her with the care of eight horses, which would have kept four squires busy; and threatened her with dire punishment if she should lose a single horse. His behavior in the corresponding adventure—the encounter with the giants—on the other hand, not only is a model of knightly manners, but also reveals for the first time Erec's capacity for disinterested compassion.

Enite does not need to tell him of the cries for help since he hears them himself, which is perhaps an indication that he is no longer completely absorbed in his own unhappiness. When he goes to investigate, he leaves Enite behind, instead of taking her with him into danger as he had done before, and on finding the distraught lady, the hero volunteers to rescue her husband, although in the encounters of section two he had not fought except when attacked himself. Overtaking the giants, he tries to persuade them to release their captive and charges them only as a last resort. In a final act of sympathy, Erec attempts to alleviate Cadoc's humiliation at being whipped by assuring him that all knights, himself included, eventually have such embarrassing experiences. It is apparent that Hartmann is intent on showing an entirely different spirit in his hero from that exhibited in the robber episode.

The most interesting use of parallel adventures to emphasize the development of hero and plot appears in the events dealing with the two counts, where many incidents of the first episode recur, usually in altered form or sequence, in the second. The squire to whom Erec gives a horse at the beginning of the earlier experience becomes the page who unwittingly brings him a horse at the end of the later one. The muted conversation at the dinner table in which Enite deceives the unnamed count reappears as the noisy exchange at the banquet where Enite defies Oringles. Her fearful soliloquy at the inn in which she disparages the value of her life compared to Erec's is expanded to the lengthy monologue on the same theme in the forest. In the earlier adventure she awakens him from sleep and they flee from the count and his men; in the later, her calls to him, whom all believe dead, revives Erec from a faint, with the result that Oringles's entire retinue flees from him. Because of the similarities of the two scenes, the chief difference stands out in bold relief. Erec, who had deliberately overburdened his wife and threatened her with death on the former occasion, asks her forgiveness on the latter—which he does not do in Chrétien's version. The change in their relationship is illustrated by two opposing symbols: the long table at the inn, with Erec seated at one end and Enite at the other, and the single horse which carries them both from Castle Limors.

The first and second Guivreiz adventures depict the initial and final steps, respectively, in the reconciliation of Erec with Enite and with society. During the first conflict of the two knights, Erec is severely wounded but manages to conquer his opponent and would have killed him if the little king had not pleaded for mercy. In the second battle Erec is defeated and would have been killed had Enite not begged for his life. Thereupon the hero exhibits true generosity, which contrasts with the murderous rage of the earlier occasion in that he exonerates Guivreiz from all blame for the encounter and assumes it himself: he has learned to lose gracefully. While the first battle is in progress, Erec speaks kindly to Enite, which he has not done since leaving Karnant; after the second battle they sleep together, thus marking the end of their estrangement. Erec's willingness to spend the following two weeks at Guivreiz's castle recovering from his injury, when compared with the overnight stay after the first battle, shows that his alienation from society is also over.[11]

The turning point in the hero's quarrel with society is the brief and reluctant exposure to the joy of the court during the short visit with Arthur and his retinue in the forest. Until then his bitter mood has been like that of Parzival between Cundrie's denunciation of him and his sojourn with Trevrizent in the wilderness. However, the friendly welcome and concern of his former companions apparently convinces Erec that neither society nor Enite, but he himself, is to blame for his downfall and that he can and should regain his reputation as an honored knight. When Hartmann places the account of Keii's schizophrenia, which is lacking in his source, here between the two halves of Erec's journey and lets us see the steward's character change from evil to good, he wishes to emphasize the change taking place in Erec, particularly as seen in his treatment of Enite. The author wants us to guess the reason for his cruelty but not condone it.

From the standpoint of dramatic effect, section three provides a light, amusing interlude between two tense and portentous series of actions. In contrast to the fierce battles of sections two and four, a comic scene is presented in which the hero with reversed spear pursues a knight who can hardly stay on his borrowed horse, and then is himself pursued by his opponent, now on foot, who is trying to get the horse back. Later comes the clever trick of Gawein and the ironical twist that Keii, who tried to bring Erec by force to Arthur's court, should be the one to bring the court to him. The fantastic account of the wondrous Famurgan ends the chapter on the level of a fairy tale.

Motifs

Certain motifs that link the separate episodes and reveal new dimensions of the underlying idea contribute to the thematic and structural unity of *Erec*. One such motif is loyalty, which is presented as an alternative to possessive love. Although the devotion of Guivreiz and Arthur's court to Erec, of Mabonagrin to his lady, and of the eighty widows to their deceased husbands shows a high degree of loyalty, the chief representative of this virtue is Enite as she appears in sections two and four. She fails at Karnant both as a queen and as a wife—as a queen by neglecting the well-being of the court in favor of private pleasure, as a wife by letting her fear of losing Erec keep her from telling him about his declining reputation—and the journey which follows gives her the opportunity to show that her attachment for her husband is more than it had appeared.[12]

Erec's reaction to the sudden revelation of his loss of honor is complex, but understandable. His shame and anger seek to fix the blame on Enite, while his love keeps him from breaking with her at once. He therefore takes her with him on his flight from disgrace, to punish her for his downfall and also to see whether he can control her and his lust for her. This is the reason why he forbids her to speak to him and why they ride, eat, and sleep apart. His fears and suspicions are later expressed in the narrator's excuse for the wrongdoing of the unnamed count. "Love was to blame for his state of mind," he says, "because we have heard that the count had been a decent and kind man of honor up to this time. . . . With Love's snare one can often catch a man too clever to be trapped otherwise. . . . No one is strong enough to escape Love once she has gained control of him." The possessive love that alienated Erec and Enite from society also alienates them from each other.[13]

During the journey Erec repeatedly commands Enite on pain of death not to speak to him and twice punishes her disobedience, but her loyalty conquers her fears and she continues to warn him of approaching danger. Enite's situation is cruelly ironic in that she now has to risk death to warn her husband and save his life because she was earlier afraid to warn him against a lesser danger. The constant growth of Erec's wrath is a result of frustration and despair, for, unlike Chrétien's hero, he is not trying to find out if Enite loves him, but whether or not she is a suitable wife for him, one who will obey him under any circumstances. He is particularly angry after the episode of the unnamed count clearly shows the danger of Enite's seductive beauty.

The beginning of a change in Erec's attitude can be seen during his first battle with Guivreiz when he responds to Enite's concern about his wound and fails to berate her because of her warning. The subsequent events, which emphasize the courtesy of Guivreiz and the Arthurian court and the brutality of the giants and Oringles, must give the hero much to think about, while he rides forth with his wife from Castle Limors, with regard to his own behavior. After he hears the full story and learns that Enite was prepared to die rather than belong to another, Erec understands that loyalty is a more desirable and reliable virtue in a wife than obedience. His newly found knowledge is confirmed a short time later when she saves his life after he is unhorsed by Guivreiz. In the meantime the reader, or listener, has learned through Enite's long soliloquy on the supposed demise of her husband the meaning of faithfulness unto death.

A second important motif which runs through *Erec* is that of the horse, perhaps the most important status symbol of the Middle Ages. Caring for a horse marked a person, of course, as a servant, while riding one was a sign of nobility. This motif, too, is primarily connected with Enite. When Erec first meets her, she takes charge of his horse—against his protests—and thus assumes the position of a stable boy. Before she leaves home, however, she is given a white palfrey which is so beautiful that she can ride up to Cardigan Castle as a highborn lady in spite of her ragged clothes. The motif next appears with Erec as he establishes a reputation for princely conduct by scorning to claim the steeds of the opponents he defeats in the jousts between Tarebron and Purin and by giving away four horses with fine saddles and bridles, a deed of considerable significance since it enables poor tournament followers to become riders.

Erec's behavior is much less regal after his failure at Karnant when he forces Enite to assume again a menial position by driving first three, then eight horses before them. Moreover, his generosity later in giving one to the young squire and the other seven to the innkeeper must be judged in the light of his position: he has nothing else with which to pay them and cannot take the horses along on his flight from the count. The comic interlude between the hero and Keii on the following day particularly stresses the horse as a status symbol. On Gawein's famous steed Keii can masquerade as a great knight, but when he is unhorsed and runs after Erec on foot, he becomes a ridiculous figure.[14]

The hero and heroine are saved from similar ignominy at Limors Castle by the unexpected appearance of the page with Erec's horse. The fact that they ride away on one mount symbolizes not only their reconciliation but also their equality. For Enite's loyalty has at last made up for the original difference in rank between her and her husband. The horse motif last appears with the splendid animal that the sisters of Guivreiz present to Enite, a gift that can be seen as a reward for trials and faithfulness, and a sign of high nobility. The illustrations on the saddle of famous people who died for love—Pyramus, Thisbe, and Dido—and one—Lavina—who suffered for love but lived on places her among the immortals.[15]

A third motif that is closely related to the theme of the story and the development of the hero is the court of Arthur. Although it does not have the central position in Hartmann's version that Chrétien gives it, the court provides a standard of knightly behavior, its praise is a measure of a knight's success, and it presents an ideal of a joyous society which is always busy with hunts, tournaments, and festivals. When Erec leaves it to pursue Iders he is regarded as a very likable but totally untried youth. He returns to a certain amount of fame, which so greatly increases during the tournament that he is ranked next to Gawein.

There is no indication whether news of the failure at Karnant has reaches Arthur's court by the time Erec next encounters it, but in any event his defeat of Keii, his wound, and his battle-scarred shield and armor would have left no doubt as to his still being a valiant warrior. What he lacks now that makes him unsuitable for courtly society is a joyful spirit. This is regained at Penefrec, and the hero can laugh with pleasure when he hears of the mighty warrior in the garden below Brandigan Castle, ride cheerfully past the sorrowing townspeople, and undertake the battle with cautious optimism. He therefore makes his final appearance at Arthur's court as the perfect knight and is praised there as such.[16]

Although the court of Arthur exemplifies the idea of a joyous court, it is not presented as a model society in all respects because it was not sufficiently close to twelfth-century German culture. The basically secular nature of the Arthurian ethic made it somewhat incompatible with medieval Christianity, and the fantastic exploits of Arthur's fairy sister suggest that his realm stood outside the area of actual experience. The ideal society was not Arthur's, but that headed at the end by the humble and God-fearing King Erec.

Style

The most important stylistic device in *Erec* is the narrator, and much of the pleasure of reading the work comes from observing the manner in which he presents his material and manipulates his fictional audience. Over one-fourth of the total verses do not directly further the plot but in one way or another are connected with the storyteller and his relationship to the tale and his listeners. He frequently mentions his source—usually as if it were oral rather than written—refers back to what he has previously said, comments on the actions, gives explanations, and asks rhetorical questions, all just to remind us that the adventures of the hero and heroine are not reality but a story which he, the recreator, is relating in his own fashion and at his own tempo to a circle of eager, sometimes impatient hearers.

The narrator varies his point of view according to the needs of the moment. Sometimes he is omniscient with regard to thoughts as well as deeds, at other times he has to fall back on his source, admit that he cannot swear to the truth of a statement, or plead ignorance on the ground that he was not there when a particular occurrence took place. The events are usually related in the past, but occasionally the narrator pretends that they are happening now and wonders what will happen next or becomes fearful and calls on God to help the hero.

Whereas Chrétien is seldom concerned with the probability of coincidences, Hartmann's playful narrator often calls attention to their unlikelihood by supporting them with obviously poor arguments or simply by saying that Erec was lucky or that a courtly God willed things that way. On occasion the narrator allows a listener to interrupt with a question or suggestion, to which he usually gives a rather superior response. However, whether the members of the audience speak up or not, he insists on their being closely involved. Addressing them in the second person 125 times, he urges them to pray for the hero's safety, dares them to search out the monsters of the sea, invites them to hunt at Guivreiz's castle, and in many ways stresses the narrator-audience relationship and the storytelling process at the expense of the illusion of the story itself.[17]

In two of the longer digressions, the accounts of Famurgan and of Enite's second palfrey, the narrator spoofs his audience with fantastic occurrences and unbelievably detailed pictorial representations in the tradition of the tall tale. Besides providing comic relief, such interludes interrupt the main action long enough to check the rapidly passing sequence of events. The retarding effect of the description of the palfrey before Erec's last battle is continued in a similar vein a few lines later when the narrator, after hinting that Brandigan Castle boded ill for the hero, refuses to tell a listener why and launches into a rather long account of the magnificent citadel with its thirty gold-capped towers, to the irritation of his impatient audience. Most of the digressions are descriptions of passive scenes, but the best, the almost incomparable flight of the wedding guests and their attendants from Limors Castle, is highly dramatic. After his vivid portrayal of struggling throngs dammed up before narrow doorways, noble warriors hiding under benches, and people spilling over the walls like hail and crawling into holes like mice, the narrator gravely excuses their fear. "As brave as I am," he says, "I would have fled had I been there." This belongs to the best humor of the Middle Ages. Although many of the narrator's intrusions are serious, so many are ironic, comical, or inconsistent that one must be cautious in using them to interpret the work.[18]

The characters of *Erec* are less loquacious than the narrator. They express themselves primarily in direct discourse, which makes up about 31 percent of the verses. This is not high compared with other works of the general period, yet is enough to add to the dramatic quality of the story, particularly of the latter part, where much of the direct discourse is concentrated. The monologues and dialogues, however, seldom advance the action, but serve mainly to characterize the speakers. The former play an important role in the work, although they are restricted mainly to Enite. Erec and the others reveal themselves for the most part in their actions.[19]

In keeping with his predilection for irony, Hartmann likes to achieve effects by strong contrasts. During the falcon contest,

Erec in old, rough armor and Enite in ragged clothing compete with the splendidly equipped Iders and his richly dressed lady. Later the fine attire of Enite contrasts with her menial task as she drives the eight horses. When Oringles argues with Enite, he repeatedly emphasizes the difference between her former low state, as he imagines it, and her present exalted one. The joy of the celebrating townspeople below Brandigan Castle suddenly turns to grief at the sight of Erec and Enite. These are only a few of the situations in which opposites—shame and honor, poverty and riches, life and death, and many others—are juxtaposed. These contrasts also appear verbally with great frequency: as nouns, adjectives, and verbs.

An element of style in *Erec* that is particularly characteristic of Hartmann is the extended metaphor. There is the game of fifteen on the head in the Iders battle, the dice game in which Erec wagers little to gain much in the Mabonagrin conflict, and the bridegroom Death of Enite's long monologue. This last metaphor grew out of the author's not uncommon tendency to personify abstractions. Others that appear are Fortune, Gossip, Love, Perfection, Want, and Wealth, all presented as ladies. The work also has some rather lengthy similes, as when the heart of Cadoc's wife is compared to a painted mirror, Erec to a ship-wrecked man in the waves of the sea, his heart to a diamond being ground by mountains of steel, and Mabonagrin's threats to the mountains which brought forth a mouse. A large number of similes make comparisons with a norm—for example, Erec acting as one does who has been injured, Enite behaving as maidens do, a belt such as women wear—but only a few of these are didactic. Many objects and situations are incomparable and lead to a frequent use of superlatives and hyperboles.[20]

A major question with regard to Hartmann's style has to do with the extent to which he intended to use certain objects, scenes, and situations that he had inherited from Chrétien as symbols. Scholars have attributed symbolic significance to many elements of *Erec*, but most of such interpretations have centered on Erec's wound, Enite's second palfrey, the Limors affair, and the events in the park below Brandigan Castle. A brief look at the last two episodes will reveal some of the problems involved. Erec's assumed death, apparent resurrection, rescue of Enite, and reconciliation with her show parallels both to Christ's passion and to the Christian death to sin, either of which might seem relevant to the plot. However, an explication based on these similarities neglects the facts that the climax of the episode is the hilarious flight from the supposed corpse and that humorous treatments of the consternation caused by men believed dead appear in medieval French and German anecdotes which Hartmann may have known.

Mabonagrin and his lady live in a park that she calls a second Garden of Eden, which links the pair with Adam and Eve and suggests that they may represent all humanity. Therefore, when Erec frees them from their self-imposed captivity, he again plays a Christ-like role. However, two obvious objections can be made to this interpretation: one is that Adam and Eve were not liberated from the Garden of Eden; the other is that the magic garden, spring, or tree defended by a fierce warrior was apparently a common folklore motif in the twelfth century. It appears in Hartmann's *Iwein*, Ulrich von Zatzikhoven's *Lanzelet Laurin,* and other medieval works. It is perhaps as likely that Chrétien and Hartmann wanted to adorn their accounts with fairy-tale elements as with religious symbolism. The situation is equally ambiguous with other elements of *Erec* that appear to have emblematic significance. In such cases it is probable that Chrétien and Hartmann were fully aware of and willing to exploit both the religious and the mythological overtones of the material they presented. Still, it is most unlikely that either intended any extended allegory.[21]

Erec soon became well known and exerted a strong influence on the narrative literature of the period and, directly or indirectly, on the entire subsequent history of the courtly verse-novel in Germany. Its popularity did not carry over into the modern period, perhaps because until fairly recently it was considered simply a tale of knightly adventure against the background of an ethical system that was meaningful only in the realm of King Arthur. Actually, however, when it portrays the individual in rebellion against society and warns of the danger of possessive love, it focuses on themes that are universal and timeless.

A Note on the Text

The text used for the following translation is *Erec von Hartmann von Aue,* edited by Albert Leitzmann, fifth edition, revised, by Ludwig Wolff (Tübingen: Niemeyer, 1972). I have supplied chapter divisions and headings. Line numbers keyed to the Leitzmann edition appear in brackets preceding paragraphs. One aspect of the line numbering may need explanation. In the standard text a fragment is inserted in a lacuna of the main manuscript between lines 4629 and 4630. This is the reason for the numbers 4629, 5 and 4629, 36 on page 84.

Notes

1. Roman Polsakiewicz, "Zur Chronologie der epischen Werke Hartmanns von Aue,"*Euphorion* 71 (1977): 82–91, reviews the theories of his predecessors with regard to the date of composition of *Erec* and suggests 1189 to 1192 or 1193. Two of the many studies of the relationships of the separate versions are those by Hendricus Sparnaay, "Zu Erec-Gereint," *Zeitschrift für romanische Philologie* 65 (1925): 53–69, which compares the French, German, and Welsh treatments, showing their similarities and differences, and Peter Wapnewski, *Hartmann von Aue,* 3d ed. (Stuttgart: Metzler, 1967), p. 40, which presents the various possibilities with regard to Hartmann's sources. Petrus W. Tax, "Der *Erek* Hartmanns von Aue: Ein Antitypus zu der *Eneit* Heinrichs von Veldeke?" in *Helen Adolf Festschrift* (New York: Ungar, 1968), pp. 47–62, indicates influences of Veldeke on Hartmann.

2. The most recent report on the manuscript and fragments, two of which have been discovered in the last few years, appears in Wolfgang Milde, " 'daz ih minne an uch suche': Neue Wolfenbütteler Bruchstücke des *Erec,*" *Wolfenbütteler Beiträge* 3 (1978): 43–58.

3. Almost all of the definitions of the theme of *Erec* fall into two groups, those that stress the proper balance between *minne* and *êre* and those that emphasize the relationship between the individual and society. However, H. Bernard Willson, "Sin and Redemption in Hartmann's 'Erec,' " *Germanic Review* 33 (1958): 14, interprets the work symbolically as "a fall from the state of joy as a consequence of sin, a period of dissimilitude, leading to redemption through rebirth." Summaries of the views of prominent scholars on the central problem appear in Walter Ohly, *Die heilsgeschichtliche Struktur der Epen*

Hartmanns von Aue (Berlin: Reuter, 1958), p. 66. More recent statements on the theme are almost unanimous in stressing the sociological implications of the work. The danger to all virtue of uncontrolled sexual passion was the object of many Latin and German *exempla* during the High Middle Ages. A discussion of these and a list of pertinent works appear in Heimo Reinitzer, "Über Beispielfiguren im *Erec*," *Deutsche Vierteljahresschrift für Literaturwissenschaft und Geistesgeschichte* 50 (1976): 600–603.

4. Dennis H. Green, "Hartmann's Ironic Praise of Erec," *Modern Language Review* 70 (1975): 795–807, states that the reference to Solomon, Absalom, Sampson, and Alexander was a deliberate ironical device of the author and cites other medieval works that mention the four as victims of women.

5. Helmut de Boor, *Die höfische Literatur: Vorbereitung, Blüte, Ausklang 1170–1250* (Munich: Beck, 1969), p. 72, regards the account of Mabonagrin's situation before Erec's arrival as Hartmann's repudiation of the overemphasis on *minne* in courtly literature.

6. Almost every *Erec* scholar who is interested in its form presents a different structural pattern. The arrangements in the following works illustrate the variety possible: Hildegard Emmel, *Das Verhältnis von 'êre' und 'triuwe' im Nibelungenlied und bei Hartmann und Wolfram* (Frankfurt: Diesterweg, 1936), p. 32; Hugo Kuhn, " 'Erec,' " in *Hartmann von Aue* (Darmstadt: Wissenschaftliche Buchgesellschaft, 1973), pp. 20–21, 31; Hansjürgen Linke, *Epische Strukturen in der Dichtung Hartmanns von Aue: Untersuchungen zur Formkritik, Werkstruktur und Vortragsgliederung* (Munich: Wilhelm Fink, 1968), pp. 107–27; Hendricus Sparnaay, *Hartmann von Aue: Studien zu einer Biographie*, 2 vols. (Tübingen: Niemeyer, 1933), 1:69; Heinz Stolte, "Der 'Erec' Hartmanns von Aue," *Zeitschrift für deutsche Bildung* 17 (1941): 299–300; and Peter Wapnewski, *Hartmann*, pp. 44–45. The highly detailed structural symmetry of the first episode is seen in Peter Wiehl, "Zur Komposition des *Erec* Hartmanns von Aue," *Wirkendes Wort* 22 (1972): 89–107.

7. The developing hero of Hartmann is contrasted with the static hero of Chrétien in Wilhelm Kellermann, "Die Bearbeitung des 'Erec-und-Enide'-Romans Chrestiens von Troyes durch Hartmann von Aue," in *Hartmann von Aue* (Darmstadt: Wissenschaftliche Buchgesellschaft, 1973), pp. 511–31.

8. Petrus Tax, "Studien zum Symbolischen in Hartmanns *Erec: Erecs ritterliche Erhöhung,*" *Wirkendes Wort* 13 (1963): 282, sees Erec as the perfect representative of the moral-religious order and his battle with Mabonagrin as representing the eternal struggle of good against evil.

9. Rolf Endres, *Studien zum Stil von Hartmanns Erec* (Munich: UNI-Druck, 1961), p. 62, suggests that Hartmann allows Enite to wear her torn clothing until she gets to Arthur's court simply in order to present a sharp contrast of rags to riches.

10. Rodney Fisher, *Studies in the Demonic in Selected Middle High German Epics* (Göppingen: Kümmerle, 1974), p. 165, considers Erec's experiences in these two series of episodes to be partly educational and partly penitential and believes that his antagonists constitute in varying degrees a demonic otherworld. Dieter Welz, "Glück und Gesellschaft in den Artusromanen Hartmanns von Aue und im 'Tristan' Gottfrieds von Strassburg," *Acta Germanica* 6 (1971): 16, sees his travels as "eine Strafexpedition gegen den Erzfeind und gefährlichsten Widersacher der höfischen Leistungsgesellschaft: gegen das Prinzip der Lust oder gegen die der wahren Ritterlichkeit feindliche Allgewalt selbstsüchtiger Sinnlichkeit."

11. Scholars are divided on the question of whether Erec thought he was being attacked on his second encounter with Guivreiz or whether he charged the king out of arrogance. Arnim Meng, *Vom Sinn des ritterlichen Abenteuers bei Hartmann von Aue* (Zurich: Juris, 1967), p. 43, advocates the former view; Wolfgang Harms, *Der Kampf mit dem Freund oder Verwandten in der deutschen Literatur bis um 1300* (Munich: Eidos, 1963), pp. 122–25, represents the latter opinion.

12. The most controversial question of *Erec* scholarship has to do with the fault of Enite with respect to her husband's failure at Karnant. Some studies absolve her entirely of blame on the ground that she could not have altered events. Barbara Thoran, " 'Diu ir man verrâten hât': Zum problem von Enîtes schuld im *Erec* Hartmanns von Aue," *Wirkendes Wort* 25 (1975): 260, maintains that Enite feared Erec might be killed in combat if she told him of his failing reputation and that, accordingly, she should not be condemned. Most scholars, however, charge Enite with neglecting both her obligations as queen and her duty to warn or guide her husband. Thomas Cramer, "Soziale Motivation in der Schuld-Sühne-Problematik von Hartmanns *Erec*," *Euphorion* 66 (1972): 105, charges her with having knowingly ignored a divinely ordained precept by marrying far above her station, a sin that required expiation. René Pérennec, "Adaptation et société: L'adaptation par Hartmann d'Aue du roman de Chrétien de Troyes: *Erec et Enide*," *Etudes germaniques* 28 (1973): 298–99, gives some support to this position. Wapnewski, *Hartmann*, pp. 53–54, says that Enite, while innocent of a particular fault, did not earn love before marriage by surmounting difficulties and therefore should do so afterwards. Cramer, "Soziale Motivation," pp. 97–99, and Hans Blosen, "Noch einmal: Zu Enites Schuld in Hartmanns *Erec*. Mit Ausblicken auf

Chrétiens Roman und das Mabinogi von 'Gereint,' " *Orbis Litterarum* 31 (1976): 83–86, give résumés of opinions by other scholars.

13. Eva-Marie Carne, *Die Frauengestalten bei Hartmann von Aue: Ihre Bedeutung im Aufbau und Gehalt der Epen* (Marburg: Elwert, 1970), pp. 89–90, presents the two most widely held views on Erec's reason for taking Enite with him on the journey: to have her share the penance for their mutual offense and to prove to her that he was still a valiant knight.

14. Jürgen Haupt, *Der Truchsess Keie im Artusroman: Untersuchungen zur Gesellschaftsstruktur im höfischen Roman* (Berlin: Schmidt, 1971), p. 134, points out that the modifications in Keii's character from heroic to evil to ridiculous as precourtly literature developed into courtly literature probably reflected a changing attitude of the aristocratic public toward his office of steward.

15. Petrus Tax, "Studien zum Symbolischen in Hartmanns 'Erec': Enites Pferd," *Zeitschrift für deutsche Philologie* 82 (1963): 29–44, discusses the symbolism of horse and saddle and its relationship to Enite.

16. The role of joy in Hartmann's courtly novels and its connection with Arthur's court is discussed in Hans Naumann and Hans Steinger, *Hartmann von Aue: Erec / Iwein* (Leipzig: Reclam, 1933), pp. 20–22.

17. An extensive and perceptive treatment of Hartmann's narrator appears in Ursula Kuttner, *Das Erzählen des Erzählten: Eine Studie zum Stil in Hartmanns 'Erec' und 'Iwein'* (Bonn: Bouvie, 1978), especially pp. 16, 33, 189, 232. Dennis H. Green, "On Damning with Faint Praise in Medieval Literature," *Viator* 6 (1975): 117–69, and "On Recognizing Medieval Irony," in *The Uses of Criticism* (Bern: Lang, 1976), pp. 11–55, shows how the dual role of narrator and commentator lends itself to irony.

18. William H. Jackson, "Some Observations on the Status of the Narrator in Hartmann von Aue's *Erec* and *Iwein*," *Forum for Modern Language Studies* 6 (1970): 66; Endres, *Studien*, p. 38; and Hans-Peter Kramer, *Erzählerbemerkungen und Erzählerkommentare in Chrestiens und Hartmanns Erec und Iwein* (Göppingen: Kümmerle, 1971), p. 73, discuss the narrator's clever manipulation of his fictitious audience and its effect on his real audience. Kramer, p. 6, reports on the views of various scholars as to whether the narrator's comments are necessarily those of the author. Kuttner, *Das Erzählen*, pp. 217–18, points to the presence of ironic humor even in the ostensibly desperate battle between Erec and Mabonagrin. Ludwig Wolff, "Hartmann von Aue: Vom *Büchlein* und *Erec* bis zum *Iwein*," *Der Deutschunterricht* 20 (1968), 2: 50–52, shows the changes that take place in Hartmann's narrator, who is less obtrusive and less important in the author's later works.

19. Herta Zutt, "Die Rede bei Hartmann von Aue," *Der Deutschunterricht* 14 (1962), 6: 72, maintains that Hartmann, when he composed *Erec*, had not yet learned the importance of the spoken word and considered it no more than a decoration to the narrative. However, Peter Wiehl, *Die Redeszene als episches Strukturelement in den Erec- und Iwein-Dichtungen Hartmanns von Aue und Chrestiens de Troyes* (Munich: Fink, 1974), pp. 88–89, shows that Hartmann devotes more than two and a half times as many verses to monologues in *Erec* as Chrétien does in his version, which indicates that Hartmann considered the monologue to be of considerable consequence in the development of his story.

20. The prominent role of sharp contrasts in Hartmann's style is shown in Ludwig Wolff, "Hartmann von Aue," *Wirkendes Wort* 9 (1959): 18, and Endres, *Studien*, p. 81. Extensive treatment of Hartmann's use of similes in *Erec* appears in Uwe Pörksen, *Der Erzähler im mittelhochdeutschen Epos: Formen seines Hervortretens bei Lamprecht, Konrad, Hartmann, in Wolframs Willehalm und in den "Spielmannsepen"* (Berlin: Erich Schmidt, 1971).

21. Among the more significant studies of *Erec's* symbolism are Willson's "Sin and Redemption," and Tax's two "Studien zum Symbolischen." Gertrud Höhler, "Der Kampf im Garten: Studien zur Brandigan-Episode in Hartmanns *Erec,*" *Euphorion* 68 (1974), 371– 419, discusses many of the Celtic and classical connotations that must be considered together with Christian-Hebraic symbolism.

Erec

CHAPTER 1

Fame and Marriage

[King Arthur and his retinue were observing an old tradition, the hunt of the white stag, according to which the one who captured the beast was to kiss the most beautiful woman at the court. Gawein had counseled against the hunt, for he feared it would cause dissension among the knights, with each maintaining that his lady was the loveliest. Queen Guinevere followed the hunters at a distance.] With her and the ladies in waiting was the hero of this story, Erec, the brave and gifted son of King Lac. They had been riding along two by two for only a short time when they saw in the distance three people riding hurriedly in their direction. In front was a dwarf, next came a beautiful, well-dressed maiden, and then a knight in the fine armor that is suitable for a noble warrior.

[14] When the queen wondered who he might be, the young Erec asked if he should find out. However, she wanted him to stay with her and chose a maiden to send, saying, "Ride over and ask who the knight and his companion are." The maiden set out as she was bidden and rode up to the dwarf.

"Good day, friend," she said politely. "Hear my request. My lady, the queen of this land, has sent me. In courtesy she directed me to greet you from her and say that she would like to know who the knight and this beautiful maiden are. No harm will be done if you tell me, since my lady's intentions are good." The dwarf wouldn't tell her and ordered her to be still and not bother him, for he didn't know what she wanted. This did not deter the maiden, and she started to ride on to ask the knight himself who he was, but the dwarf blocked the way. Then Erec

31

and the queen saw him use a whip he was holding to strike her shamefully on the head and hands so that welts were raised.

[59] With this answer she returned to her lady and let her see how violently she had been struck. The queen lamented bitterly that this should happen right before her eyes, and Erec thought that it was dishonorable of the knight to look on and do nothing while his dwarf struck the maiden. He said, "I'll ride over and find out for you."

[73] "Go then," replied the lady, and Erec left at once. When he was close enough for the dwarf to hear him, he asked, "Tell me, little fellow, why did you strike the girl? You have acted very badly, and common courtesy should have kept you from it. Tell me the name of your master. My lady would like to know who he and the pretty maiden are."

"Hold your tongue," spoke the dwarf. "I'll tell you only that you'll get the same thing. Why did she want to know who my lord is? You people are fools to ask so much about him today; it can indeed do you harm. If you want me to spare you, then be on your way and quickly, you loathsome creature."

[95] Erec tried to go past, but the dwarf wouldn't allow it and struck him with the whip, just as he had done to the maiden. Erec would have liked to have gotten revenge, but he wisely controlled his rage: he wore no more armor than a woman, and the knight would have killed him. He had never been so distressed as at this blow, and nothing had ever shamed him more than having the queen and her ladies witness this insult.

[109] After being struck, he rode back greatly mortified and, with flaming cheeks, lamented his sorrow: "Lady, I can't deny it, for you saw it yourself. In your presence I suffered greater dishonor than has ever befallen any of my peers. To be struck so disgracefully by such a small man and have to endure it makes me so ashamed that I shall never dare face you or these young ladies again. I don't know what good my life is except to make up for what has happened right before your eyes. If I don't die at once, I shall try. Lady, be so kind as to let me depart. May heaven's King keep you in high esteem. You will never see me again if I don't avenge myself on the man whose dwarf gave me these welts. Should God grant me such honor and good fortune

that I am successful, as indeed I hope, I'll return after three days—if my health permits."

[144] The queen was distressed that, young as he was, he should ride into great danger and asked him not to make the journey, but he persisted in begging leave to go until at last she granted it. The youthful lord thought it would be too far for him to ride back to where his armor was, that he would never return with it in time: no matter how he hurried, they would surely get away from him. He therefore hastened after them as he was.

[160] Setting out at a fast pace, he came at once on the tracks of those who had mistreated him and soon caught sight of them. However, he didn't try to catch up, but followed at such a distance that he could see them without being noticed. He acted as one does who has suffered injury and takes great care to even things up in a suitable manner. On the way they never got out of his sight throughout the long day until evening. Then he saw gleaming before him a castle named Tulmein that belonged to Duke Imain, into which the knight in front of him rode. He was well received, as one should be in the house of a friend, and in a manner befitting the host.

[181] I'll tell you why he came there with his lady friend. The two previous years, if the report is true, Duke Imain had held a festival, which was now to be celebrated a third time and was to be repeated each year for the diversion of his people. He admitted everyone to the affair. Poor and rich alike, old and young came to his festivity—when they heard of it—because of the fine entertainment. In the middle of a meadow the duke placed a small falcon on a silver perch which rested on a high stand. The falcon was to go to the lady who won the beauty contest here. The knight had taken it twice and had come to get it a third time. If he succeeded, he was to keep it in honor from then on without further contests. They say that many women there were prettier than the knight's lady, but this showed how brave he was: he was so feared that he could just seize it. He didn't need to fight, for no one dared oppose him.

[218] Erec knew nothing of these things and had ridden after the knight to try his fortune only because of the injury done him. It was becoming dark when he rode into the small market town

below the castle, which he avoided in order to escape the attention of the man he had followed. When he went to see who would be kind enough to put him up for the night, he met a large throng: all of the houses were filled with guests, and he could find no one anywhere who would take him in. Moreover, he had nothing with which to pay for a lodging. He had suddenly decided to start out and had made no preparation for the journey, as I have already told you. Now he was quite concerned, for he had only his clothing and his palfrey. Also he was a stranger there, so no one spoke to him or looked at him in a friendly manner, although the streets were filled with people amusing themselves, as is usual at festivals.

[250] Thus forsaken, he rode until he noticed far ahead an old ruin. Because it was so difficult to find lodgings, he turned into a road that brought him to it: as he couldn't stay anywhere else, he decided to spend the night there. He looked at the castle and believed it deserted, which pleased him. He thought, "Things are going all right now, for I can stay inside in some nook until daylight, since I haven't anything better. Surely no one will object; I can easily see that it is vacant."

[270] When he had entered and was looking for a small recess suitable for him to stay in, he saw sitting there an old man with snow-white, well-groomed hair that had been carefully combed down over his shoulders. He wore a coat and hat of sheepskin, as the story goes, both as good as his affairs permitted: he was not rich. Yet the manner of the man who was sitting there in the ruin, leaning on a cane, was very refined and like that of a nobleman. Erec was disappointed, for he was afraid that he would be sent away once more. He at once tied his palfrey and laid his cloak on it. Then he stretched out his hands, as one who is well bred, and went to the old man. "Sir, I need lodgings," he said uneasily and blushed with embarrassment at the request. But when the man heard him, he answered, "You are welcome to what I can offer," and Erec the son of King Lac thanked him.

[308] The only other occupants of the castle were a maiden—the most beautiful one of whom we have ever heard—and the mistress of the house. The gentility of the man could be seen by his taking in a guest when he himself was so poor. Calling for the maiden, he said, "Go, my daughter, and care for the palfrey

of this lord who does us the honor of being our guest. Provide for
it well, so that I shall not need to reprove you."

[322] "I shall do it, sir," she replied. The maiden's figure was
lovely, but the green dress she wore was threadbare and tattered. The shift beneath it was discolored and also torn in places,
so that her body gleamed through as white as a swan. They say
that no other maiden was so perfectly formed: she lacked only
wealth to be an excellent match. Her body shone through her
faded clothing like a white lily among black thorns. I suppose
that God showed his greatest skill with regard to beauty and
grace when he created her.

[342] Erec was sorry to put her to any trouble and said to her
father, "Let us excuse the young lady, because I don't suppose
she has ever done this before. It is a task for which I am better
suited myself."

"It is well to let the host have his way," answered the old man.
"Since we have no stable boys, it is right that she should do it."
The maiden hurried to do her father's bidding. Her white hands
carefully looked after the palfrey: I fancy that, if God himself
were riding about here on earth, he would be glad to have a
groom like this one. In spite of her shabby clothing, I am sure
that no one ever had a more charming squire than Erec had
when she was caring for his palfrey. It was justly pleased to get
its fodder from such a stable boy.

[366] The guest was entertained here according to their
means. Beautiful rugs; the finest bedding on them, all covered
with samite in which there was so much gold that one man could
not lift it and needed three more to lay it out; a costly, brightly
decorated taffeta quilt spread over it in the splendor of great
lords—these were not to be found that evening by the fire. To be
sure, they could afford clean straw, and they were satisfied with
simple bedding covered with a white sheet. An abundance of fine
food was there—the best that a wise man could imagine—but it
did not appear on the table. They were content with the good
intention which prevailed: this is the surety of all kindness.

[396] Now you shall hear who this old man was whose poverty
did not keep him from giving the stranger a cordial welcome.
Once he had enjoyed greater wealth and honor. Indeed, he had
been a mighty count before stronger peers had seized his

hereditary possessions. He had done nothing wrong—no evil deed had brought him to this want—it was caused by war. The superior strength of his foes had robbed him of everything, and he now had so little of his former riches and esteem left that he could not keep a single manservant. He and his noble wife bore poverty in their old age with wisdom and, whatever they did without, concealed their need as well as they could beneath courtesy so that it would not be noticed. As a matter of fact, no one knew that they were destitute. The hardships suffered because of poverty seemed to the master of the house as sweet as honey compared to the shame he felt.

[428] The old man's name was Koralus, his wife's was Karsinefite, and his daughter's was Enite. Whoever would not have felt sorry for this needy family of nobles would have been hard as a stone. The young lady's uncle was the ruler of the land, the Duke Imain who was holding the festival: she was not of lowly birth.

[440] We shall now also tell how their story was revealed. When the palfrey was cared for, the host said, "I shall be glad to help you pass the time." So Erec, still greatly distressed at the insult he had received, asked the meaning of the large crowd he had seen in the market town, and the man told him about the situation—about the festival and the falcon contest—just as I have described it to you. When his host had explained this, Erec questioned him concerning the knight, asking if he knew who the man was who had ridden in front of him and had gone into the other castle—as I related to you earlier—but said nothing of his own trouble.

[463] "The whole country knows him," the old man answered; "his name is Iders the son of Niut." He went on to tell the purpose of Iders's journey, that he had come with his lady to claim the falcon. As soon as Erec heard this, he made further inquiries until at last his host revealed his own situation.

After he had finished, the young man stood up and spoke, "I beg you, lord and host, to favor my request. Since your affairs are thus, I would like help and advice. Trusting in your kindness, let me tell you that I have received an injury from this knight which I shall always lament unless I even the score. His dwarf gave me a hard blow that I could not avenge since his master was in armor and I was not. The dwarf took advantage of this. I had to endure great shame then, and my heart will forever bemoan it if God does not give me a chance to get vengeance. Hoping for such good fortune, I followed him here—as I told you. I now ask for your support: aid and deliverance, sir, are entirely in your hands.

[499] "I'll tell you what I have in mind. I already have a good horse, and, if you could somehow help me to get armor, he wouldn't get by without a fight. You could let me ride to the festival with your daughter Enite, and I would claim that she was more beautiful than the knight's lady and should take the falcon. See what you can do, with the understanding that I am to marry her if I win the victory. You should not decline in the belief that I would not be a good match, for it will indeed be to her honor. I'll tell you who my father is: King Lac. And I shall make all I have subject to her—people, land, myself—that she may rule them."

[525] The eyes of the old man then became dim with hidden grief: this proposal saddened his heart and brought him so close to tears that he could hardly answer. "Sir," he replied, "for God's sake do not mock me. Your words are unfeeling. God has ordained for me what he wished, and my life is not what it should have been. I will accept this from almighty God, who can make the rich man poor and the poor man rich whenever he pleases, as can be seen in my case. Still, I pray you in God's name not to jest, for, unless I am quite mistaken, your asking for my daughter's hand was only a joke. You can indeed forego taking her as a wife, since she has nothing. But however great my present need, you can believe me this: there was a time when your father, King Lac, called me his friend. In fact, we were knighted together in his land."

[560] Erec blushed at the reproach and said, "Sir, why do you think I was jesting? You should not believe that but take my words seriously. What good would scoffing do me now? As truly as I pray God to help my body and soul, so truly I want your daughter to be my wife. I'll let you wait no longer than the end of the combat at this festival, if with your help my affair turns out well. You lament her poverty: say no more about it. I shall not hold it against you, because I can easily do without her dowry.

Besides, it would be petty of me to let property determine my choice. Remember that. However, since the combat is to take place in the morning, let us delay no longer. My honor depends entirely on you—and you may be sure that I shall do as I have promised."

[588] The old man was happy when he heard this and said, "Since your intentions are thus, I can tell you that we have here some splendid armor which is both light and strong. My poverty could never bring me to such despair that I would sell it. I kept it with the thought that a friend might need it, and, because of this, I would have lent it to him. As long as God allowed me— until old age conquered me and took away my strength—I was always ready to wear it myself in support of a friend. Now the armor will save us the embarrassment of having to ask a stranger for aid. I have also kept both a shield and a spear." Erec thanked the old man and asked to be shown the armor so that he could see if it fit him and was neither too tight nor too heavy. It was indeed suitable and light, which greatly pleased him.

[621] The day on which they were to go to the festival soon dawned. When the sun was high, they rode to Tulmein, where Duke Imain—surprised to see them—gave them a hearty welcome. They took him aside, told why they had come and what Erec intended to do, and asked his aid. "I'll tell you what I'll do," said the duke. "Because of your bravery and the honor of my niece, dear guest, I'll place my good will and all I have at your disposal: take my advice and let me dress her better."

[641] "That shall not be," objected Erec. "Whoever judges a woman only by her clothing is greatly deceived. One should decide on the basis of her person, not her dress, whether or not a woman is beautiful. Be that as it may, today I'll show the knights and ladies that my spear and sword could ensure her high praise if she were as bare as my hand and blacker than coal, or I'll die in the attempt."

[657] "God send you good fortune," replied Duke Imain. "You may be certain that your bravery will win you everything good." While speaking thus, they came to the chapel and heard a mass of the Holy Spirit, as those always do who like jousting and look forward to knightly deeds. By then a meal was ready and they were served very courteously. Afterwards each sought out the

amusement he preferred, according to his taste and mood, on the meadow where the falcon was perched. All were watching to see when Iders the son of Niut would go with his lady and take the falcon, as he had done before. Then they saw Erec come up with Lady Enite by his side. He led her to the falcon and, speaking loudly enough for the knight to hear, he said, "Lady, untie the cords and put it on your hand, for you are without question the most beautiful one here."

Iders was annoyed and spoke up scornfully, "Let the falcon alone! You won't be as lucky as that, you beggar. Have you lost your senses? Leave it to one who is more worthy and has a right to it, my lady here. She deserves it."

[700] "Sir Knight," said Erec, "the past two years you have taken the falcon unjustly. You can be sure that you won't get it again unless it is awarded to you. Knightly combat shall decide the matter between us."

"Youth," replied the other, "if your life means anything to you, withdraw this childish challenge now, for otherwise you will soon give it up under worse conditions, in mortal danger. I'll tell you beforehand what will happen to you. I won't have any pity: when I defeat you—as doubtless I shall—I don't intend to accept any ransom for your life. Whoever advised you in this is one who is happy to see you fail."

[724] "Sir," spoke Erec, "I have said what I have to say and shall change nothing." They parted at once and armed themselves: the knight as he wished, Erec with what he had.

Iders was well equipped, since he had prepared himself for combat as one should. His spears were brightly colored, the crest of his helmet was decorated, and his horse was decked out in a splendid caparison—which Erec didn't have. His surcoat was just as fine, of grass-green samite that was adorned all around with costly trimming, and his armor too deserved high praise—so we are told. He looked like a noble knight. Erec also rode up. His shield was old and heavy, long and broad; his spear was thick and hard to wield; and he and his horse were only half covered by the armor that his old father-in-law had lent him. All the people there spoke with one voice: "May God be with you today," and fortune did not refuse him its aid.

[755] A wide ring was cleared for them at once. Young Erec's

bravery gave him great strength—which made him well fitted for combat—and both knights were moved with fierce anger. Their legs flew as they spurred their horses forward. The arrogance of the one deceived him then, because he thought he was charging at a mere child. However, when they met, he indeed learned that Erec had a warrior's spirit, for the knight's shield was driven against his head with such violence that he was stunned and almost fell from the saddle. This had never happened to him before. The joust was so fierce that the horses were thrown back on their haunches and the broken spear shafts flew from their hands over the tops of the shields. The blow Iders received was unlike any he had known until then.

[782] After they had jousted five times in a most praiseworthy manner—with neither missing once, but striking so hard that their spears splintered—Erec had only a single spear left, which put him at a great disadvantage. He had kept the old one of his father-in-law for the last charge because the shaft was thick and solid. He had also wisely saved his strength till then. When he took up the spear, which matched well the heavy shield in front of him, he rode a short distance out of the ring to where he saw Enite weeping and spoke over the shield: "Cheer up, noble maid, for I am still quite undaunted. There will be an end to your worries."

[807] He then turned his horse and, couching his spear, rode toward the knight, who was also ready. They dashed at each other with all the speed they could get from their horses and met with such force that the knight's surcingle, breastplate, and two saddle girths broke: never before had he been in such distress. Although he was valiant, Erec threw him from his horse and made him the laughingstock of the people there.

[824] When Erec succeeded in unhorsing the knight, he stopped at some distance from him so that no one could say that he had shamefully killed the man while he was lying prostrate. He wanted a better name than that. Erec dismounted and ordered the knight to get up. Then they went at each other and fought like two noble warriors. Fire flew from their helmets. They struggled as befits people who are driven by bitter necessity, for they had set a high value on victory. No less than life and honor was at stake, and they acted accordingly.

[845] They had fought manfully for some time when Iders struck Erec so fiercely on the helmet that the youth fell to his knees. Enite was greatly alarmed at this and began to bewail her lover, for she thought the blow had killed him. However, he sprang up, threw his shield on his back in fury, and, wielding his sword with both hands, fought like a madman. He cut the knight's shield to pieces, then hewed it from his hand, but his foe, undaunted, answered him blow for blow and paid back what had been lent like one who wishes to keep his credit good. Both were playing a game called fifteen on the head, at which one can easily lose; still, they were sometimes paid in advance and above what was due.

[872] They threw the dice in fury. Whoever collected the interest on the pledges could well have received a wound a yard long. Many bets were made and all were raised. Neither wanted to give up, for to do so would have cost both life and honor. Sparks flying, the contest thus continued with such heat from morning till noon that the two at last had nothing more to wager and were exhausted. They did not have the means to make bets and could no longer move their arms as before. They had worn themselves out with fighting and rage to the point where they were unable to go on: they were so weary that their blows fell like those of a woman and did no harm.

[897] "Stop, good knight," said Iders then. "What we are now doing discredits chivalry and merits no praise. This feeble struggle is not worthy of brave warriors: we are fighting disgracefully, with unmanly blows. If you would not think it cowardice, I would suggest that we leave off and rest a while." Erec was pleased at his words, and, taking off their helmets, they both sat down to rest.

[913] When they felt refreshed, they went up to each other and continued their old game—as I shall tell you presently. They contended with great cleverness, new strength, and like skill: even after a long time neither the well versed nor the novices among the onlookers could tell who had the advantage by a single point. The uncertainty as to who would win lasted until the young Erec began to think about the shame and distress the knight's dwarf had caused him on the moor. This and the sight of the lovely Enite helped him to fight with great power, for he

became fully twice as strong. With an eager hand he took control
of the other's helmet, and although the knight made the best
throws a player could wish for, Erec never let him escape from
the rain of blows and maintained the attack with such zeal that
his adversary finally lost the game and lay defeated before him.
The whiplash was avenged.

[951] When he tore off the knight's helmet, Erec also loosened
the hood underneath as if he were to be killed unless he was
willing to ask for mercy. "For God's sake, noble knight, have
pity on me," begged the man. "Do honor to all women by sparing
my life and in courtesy remember that I have never done you
any great harm. It would not hurt you to let me live."

[964] To this Erec replied, "How can you say that now? You
are needlessly making fun of me. You wanted nothing but my
death: the victory you expected and your arrogance wouldn't
satisfy you. Indeed, you weren't going to accept any ransom for
my life. But God was kind to me, and the matter turned out
differently. See, now I don't have to pay for my life. However God
may preserve it otherwise, I am at least safe from you. If you had
been a little less insolent to me, you would be better off. Your
own arrogance brought you down today and gave you sorrow as
a companion."

[986] "What do you mean?" asked the knight; "I didn't earn
your enmity. Truly, I never saw you before." But Erec said,
"Because of me you feel the shame today that was mine yesterday when, because of you, I had to endure disgrace that cut me to
the heart. And I predict that your dwarf's strength and bad
manners will never profit you enough to make up for the harm
they have just done you."

[1000] "If I am to blame for any injury you have suffered,"
answered the knight, "I am sorry. In any case your bravery here
has punished me for this offense. Spare my life, and I will
compensate you fully for whatever I have done for which I
should make amends." Erec pitied him and spoke thus: "I'll let
you live, which you would not have done for me." The knight
then promised to perform such service as was demanded in
exchange for his life.

[1018] After the vow was made, Erec bade him stand up, and,
when both had bared their heads, he said, "I require that you do

one thing for me: my lady the queen must be honored to make up for the insult she received. You showed much enmity toward her and caused her greater distress than she had ever known before. She laments this bitterly, and you must atone for it. Yesterday at about this time your dwarf struck one of her maidens and later struck me, too, so that I got this welt. See, it is I, the same man. And I would have followed you forever rather than have you escape my vengeance.

[1039] "That your dwarf should give me this mark under the eye—you can't deny that it is there—and that he should be so rude as to strike the maiden are matters which I will not simply accept, and he shall be properly punished. I'll tell you why: his bad manners pleased him so much that they deserve a reward. I'll not consider myself, but say only that he should not have done it to the maiden. I'll take from this dog a suitable forfeit, his hand, to teach him to show more honor to ladies from now on."

[1056] The noble youth did not really intend to do this, but only wanted to warn the dwarf against any more such acts, and it did not take much pleading to talk him out of it. Nevertheless, a just penalty was imposed. Erec ordered two men to stretch the dwarf out on a table and whip him with two sturdy switches: the marks could be seen on his back at least twelve weeks later. He was punished for his brutality until blood ran down from him, and when they heard of his deed, everyone agreed that he had gotten what he deserved. The dwarf's name was Maliclisier.

[1078] Annoyed at the knight's lingering, Erec then spoke to him: "I don't know why you are waiting here and not riding off to the queen. You should have left before now. You are to deliver yourself up to her and do as she commands. Tell her who you are, about our fight, and that Erec the son of King Lac sent you. I'll come when I can, perhaps tomorrow: it is only seven leagues. Now remember your promise." The knight, his lady, and the dwarf then rode off toward the court of Arthur.

[1089] In the meantime the king had again left his castle of Cardigan and gone into the countryside where they were hunting the stag—as you were told earlier—and had caught it with his own hands. The right which went with this feat had therefore fallen to him: he could kiss anyone he wished of all the maidens. The king wanted to make use of it, as was the custom,

as soon as they returned to Cardigan. However, after his right
was conceded, the queen asked him not to exercise it until she
had told him all her experiences of that same day: what had
happened on the moor and how the knight had offended her.
[1124] "My dear," she said, "I have a grievance to present. My
maiden was struck, just as I told you, and also Erec the son of
King Lac. Distressed by this whiplash, he parted from me on the
moor, saying, 'Believe me, my lady, you will never again see me
in Britain unless I avenge my shame. But if I can get vengeance,
I'll return in three days.' Sir, that will be tomorrow. I am hope-
ful, but worried, about the youth and his affair. I couldn't restrain him. May God send him back to us! My dear, for my sake
as well as his I request that you not bestow the kiss until you
hear how things have gone with him. I would like to have him
present, too. I ask you to wait only until tomorrow morning: if he
is successful, he will be here."
    [1150] This appeal was made at Cardigan Castle soon after
Gawein and his friend Keii, the lord high steward, had left the
ladies and, hand in hand, had gone out beyond the walls to look
around. When they saw a knight ride out of the distant forest
and approach in haste, they quickly informed the queen, who
got up at once and went with her ladies to a window in order to
see who was coming. They and the knights stood there side by
side, in doubt as to who the rider might be.
    [1171] Then the queen spoke up: "If my heart and the distance
do not deceive me, it is indeed the man whom Erec followed. See,
there are three of them: the dwarf and his lady are riding with
him. It is he and no one else. He looks as if he were coming from a
battle. You can see that his shield has been hewn away almost
down to the boss and his armor is covered with blood. I tell you
truly, either he has killed Erec and has come to boast of his
victory or, as I fervently hope, the youth has sent him here as a
defeated knight in order to honor our court." Everyone agreed
with the queen that either might be the case.
    [1196] Just then, before they had finished speaking, Iders rode
over the courtyard of Cardigan to a broad and rather high stone
which had been placed in front of the castle steps so that King
Arthur could dismount or sit there. After looking around for a
better place, the knight dismounted at the stone. When grooms

had taken their horses, he, his lady, and the dwarf went courteously before the queen, who received him in a stately manner. The knight fell at her feet and said, "Great lady, in kindness assume authority over me, a man to whom God has denied honor. I have acted thoughtlessly toward you and for no cause but my own malice. I followed the leading of a foolish heart and should therefore make amends to you.

[1225] "I regret it now that it is too late: like the hare caught in the net, I am wary at the wrong time. I am very sorry about it. The saying that arrogance can easily bring one to harm is indeed true. I have realized this and come to the end of it, for he almost took my life as well as my fame. I admit my fault, that I caused you grief: I am the one whom you met yesterday on the moor. It proved unfortunate for me that I let my dwarf be so brutal as to strike the maiden. Erec the son of King Lac has made me atone bitterly for the insolence of the whiplash, as my offense required of him. He defeated me in combat and sent me here, my lady, to win your pardon for the misdeed and place myself fully in your service. Moreover, I can tell you that you need not be concerned about him, for he is coming himself tomorrow and bringing with him a maiden of whom none can truthfully say that he has seen one more beautiful."

[1260] King Arthur and the queen were very pleased with the news and thanked God that Erec, young as he was, had been so successful and that his first knightly combat had ended so fortunately and laudably. Only a very jealous person would have begrudged him this good luck, and no one was better liked by the members of the court. From childhood on, he had performed so many services for them that all were happy about it. "Your punishment shall be less than you have earned," said the queen. "It is my will that you remain here as a part of our retinue." There could be no disputing her decision. After these words the king said to the knights, "We should arrange a splendid reception for Erec as a reward. It is our duty to extend every honor to a man who really deserves it, and what he has done merits our praise." Everyone agreed with this.

[1294] When it happened thus—as you have already heard— that Erec did so well at Tulmein Castle and defeated Iders, who had always shown himself to be a valiant warrior, and when

Lady Enite's claim was upheld by the combat, all the people
there rejoiced at his good fortune and maintained that he was
without doubt the noblest man ever to come to their country. No
one was vexed at his victory, and everybody praised his bravery.
In his honor they expanded the festivities: at one place a large
bohort began, at another there was dancing. Duke Imain took
off Erec's armor, and the young Enite laid his head in her lap so
that he could rest from the battle.

[1320] She acted very shy, as maidens do, and said little to
him. That is the way they are: at first they are as bashful and
timid as children, but later they learn to know what suits them
and to like what at first seemed difficult. They find that they
would rather have a fond kiss, when they can get it, than a blow
and a good night than a bad day.

[1334] Then Duke Imain asked Erec if he and his lady would
be so kind, for friendship's sake, as to spend the night with him
and asked his brother-in-law to give up his guest. However, Erec
declined, saying, "Sir, how could I do this? Should I forsake the
host who treated me very well? Yesterday he and your sister
received me, a complete stranger, most cordially, and I must
repay them. I know that he did all he could for me, even giving
me his daughter. Therefore do not be offended because I do not
leave him. If I should do so, he might well think that I hold his
poverty against him, which, God knows, is not the case. I shall
be very glad to be his guest and shall also show him my loyalty
in another way: if we both live for six months and I do not lose
my wealth, I'll make him rich. I'll hold fast to my resolve and see
to it that he becomes as well-off as he ever was."

[1364] "Since you won't stay with me," replied Duke Imain,
"we shall go with you." Erec and his father-in-law thanked him.
Then they arose, took each other by the hand, and, with Enite
between them, went to the castle. She was happy because the
falcon which had been won was on her hand; this was indeed
reason enough for joy. The maiden thus had the good fortune to
gain a notable honor, but she was, of course, even more pleased
with the beloved husband whom she had gotten that day.

[1386] A man who enjoyed amusement was well entertained
then, for there was great jubilation in all the places where
guests were lodging. Erec saw countless knights and ladies that

evening, because everyone at the festival was invited to come to his quarters. Enite's father could not have paid for this, and the duke had to take over: plenty of food was carried from his castle.

[1400] When the sun rose on the following day, Erec did not want to wait longer. He spoke of his lack of time and said that he had to take Enite and ride back. Her uncle asked if he might dress her better, but Erec declined the offer. The duke also wanted to give him gold and silver, which the knight rejected, saying that he did not need them. Moreover, he would take neither horses nor clothing, only a palfrey suitable for Enite to ride. It came from one of her cousins, a girl who, it is said, was closely related to the duke and lived at his castle. She begged Erec most kindly until at last he accepted it from her.

[1423] You should know that no one in the world ever had a more beautiful palfrey. It was ermine-white with a broad chest, long flanks, fine feet and back, and a curly mane which hung far down. It was neither too fat nor too thin, too large nor too small. It held its head high and was calm, gentle, and easy to ride. My, how smoothly and swiftly it bore one at an amble across the fields: it never stumbled but moved as nicely as a ship. The saddle was in keeping with the palfrey. The metal parts were of red gold—but why should I tell you at great length how it was made? I must leave out much, for it would take too long if I described it fully. Therefore, I'll end my praise by saying only that the girths were of silk and gold thread.

[1454] When the palfrey was brought to Erec, there was no further delay. In saying good-bye Enite wept freely, as one might expect of a maiden, because she was leaving her dear mother to ride into a strange land. And the mother prayed: "Almighty and merciful God, please care for my child!" The blessing truly was somewhat longer. Parting brought both of them to tears and also the father, who implored our Lord God to look after his daughter. Erec told Koralus to follow the directions of the messenger whom he would send, for he, Erec, intended to bring the old man's poverty to an end. In hope of this the latter was happy and bowed deeply. The two then took leave of all the company and rode off alone, for Erec did not want anybody to accompany them. He gave the people his best wishes and asked that they remain there.

[1484] As soon as Erec and Enite were on the heath, he began to look at his bride, and she—shyly, but often—looked at him. Her heart was full of love as they continued to exchange fond glances. Indeed, each became more and more pleased with the other; neither enmity nor hatred found a dwelling place there, because good will and loyalty had taken full possession of them. They rode swiftly since Erec had promised to return that day.

[1501] From the story of the queen and the report of the knight who had come there after Erec had defeated him, all the knights knew just when the youth was to arrive and had their horses ready. His bravery was then rewarded as they rode forth with King Arthur from the castle—Gawein, Persevaus, King Iels of Galoes, Estorz son of King Ares, Lucans the cupbearer, and the entire retinue—to receive him sociably with knightly revelry, as one does when one finds a good friend who was lost. At the same time my lady the queen was walking across the courtyard to greet him. Happy with the outcome of his adventure, she bade Erec welcome and then took charge of Enite, saying, "Lovely maiden, you must get some other clothing."

[1532] The noble lady led Enite to her private rooms. Water was heated, and she relaxed from the journey with a fine bath. Later the queen dressed her dear guest, for much rich clothing lay ready. With her own hands she sewed the maiden into a white silk chemise and put over it a splendid, well-cut gown in the French style which just fit. It was of green samite with span-wide borders of gold thread on both sides, as is proper. Around Enite's waist was placed an Irish belt of a sort which ladies like to wear, and at her throat was fastened a gleaming ruby brooch the width of a hand, but its luster could not compare with the radiant beauty of the maiden.

[1566] The queen covered the gown with a mantle of like splendor. It was of silk and gold fabric with sable trimming at the wrists and a lining of ermine. Enite's hair was bound with a rather broad, shining ribbon—no finer was ever made—which went crosswise over her head. Her clothing was costly, and she was noble. Dame Want veiled her head in great confusion, because she had brazenly been robbed of her lodgings. She had to withdraw and flee from the house as Wealth moved in. Since the maiden had looked so beautiful even in shabby clothing—so they say—she now, in such splendid dress, was really worthy of praise. I would gladly extol her as she deserves, but I am not wise enough and would fail: my skill is not that great. Moreover, so many wise lips have devoted themselves to lauding women that I would not know what praise to devise in order to equal that already heaped on others. Lacking experience, I cannot do her justice, but shall nevertheless proclaim her beauty as best I can and as I have heard it: Lady Enite was without question the loveliest maiden ever to enter the king's court.

[1611] The queen took her cordially by the hand and led her to where the king was sitting in his usual place at the Round Table in the company of many noble knights. One of them was the most highly acclaimed of all who ever sat there, at that time or later—so the rest maintained—for it was said that he never did anything blameworthy. He had so many virtues that one still counts him among the finest men at the Round Table: the noble Gawein well deserved his seat. Next to him sat Erec the son of King Lac. Then came Lanzelot of Arlac, Gornemanz of Groharz, Coharz the Handsome, Lais the Bold, Meljanz of Liz, Maldwiz the Wise, the rash Dodines, and the noble Gandelus. Beside Gandelus was Esus, and after him came Brien, Iwein the son of King Urien, Iwan of Lonel (who was always quick to seek fame), Iwan of Lafultere, Onam of Galiot, and Gasosin of Strangot.

[1648] Also sitting there were the Knight with the Golden Bow, Tristram, Garel, Bliobleherin, Titurel, Garedeas of Brebas, Gues of Strauz, Baulas, Gaueros of Rabedic, Lis of Quinte Carous (the son of the king of Ganedic), Isdex of Mount Sorrow, Ither of Gaheviez, Maunis, Galez the Bald, Grangodoans, Gareles, Estorz the son of Ares, Galagaundris, Galoes, the son of Duke Giloles, Lohut the son of King Arthur, Segremors, Praueraus, Blerios, Garredoinechshin, Los, Trimar the Young, Brien the Quick-Tongued, Equinot the son of Count Haterel, Lernfras the son of Gain, Henec Suctellois the son of Gawin, Le, Gahillet, Maneset of Hochturasch, Batewain the son of King Cabcaflir, [lacuna] Galopamur the son of Isabon, Schonebar, Lanfal, Brantrivier, Malivliot of Katelange, Barcinier, the faithful Gothardelen, Gangier of Neranden and his brother Scos, the valiant Lespin, Machmerit, Parcefal of Glois, Seckmur of Rois, Inpripalenot, Estravagaot, Pehpimerot, Lamendragot,

Oruogodelet, Affibla the Merry, Arderoch, Amander, Ganatu-
lander, Lermebion of Jarbes, and the son of Mur with the Four-
fold Armor. Now I have named for you the entire noble band.
There were one hundred and forty of them, to be exact.

[1698] Toward this group the queen led the perfect beauty,
Enite. If the red of roses were to pour over the white of lilies and
the two flow together, it would resemble her except for the lips,
which were like roses alone. No lovelier woman was ever seen.
When she passed through the doorway and saw them seated
there, she was at first painfully embarrassed. She lost color and
then became red and pale in turn at the sight, as I shall tell you:
if the sun in broad daylight is shining in full splendor and
suddenly goes behind a thin and narrow cloud, the glow is no
longer as bright as it was. In like manner Enite's shyness caused
her distress for a short time. As she approached, her beautiful
face took on more color and was even more charming than
before. How well those blushes became her! They were caused by
her embarrassment: until then she had never seen so many
splendid knights sitting together.

[1736] When Enite entered the hall, those at the Round Table
were startled by her beauty and, forgetting themselves, stared
at the maiden. There was no one who would not have declared
her to be the fairest woman he had ever seen. The king went to
Enite, took her by the hand, and seated her at his one side and
the noble queen at the other. He then thought it time to bring
the dispute of the knights to a quick end. You know—for I have
already told you—that the king was to make use of the right he
had won by his good fortune in capturing the white stag, the
right to kiss the lips of the one whom all believed to be the most
beautiful woman at the court. At the request of the queen he had
waited until this moment, but it was needless to delay longer
since Enite was without question the most beautiful woman
there, and in the rest of the world as well.

[1766] I'll tell you just how her beauty excelled that of the
others. When the stars shine brightly on a dark night so that
they can be clearly seen, one rightly declares that they are
charming, if nothing more lovely appears. But as soon as the
moon comes up, one considers the beauty of the stars to be
nothing in comparison, even though they would seem worthy of

praise if the moon were not present to darken them with its gleaming splendor. In like manner Enite outshone the ladies of the court. So the king no longer hesitated to observe the custom passed on by his father, Utpandragon, which was to take the kiss only from her on whom the knights agreed and from no one else. He stood up and received his reward from his kinsman's bride, which he could do without angering anyone because of their relationship.

[1797] A great deal of celebrating now took place at Cardigan Castle in honor of Erec and Enite as everybody tried to outdo the others in merriment. Where could one find greater pleasure than they enjoyed all of the time there?

Then the noble Erec remembered the poverty of his father-in-law and sent a messenger to him with riches that King Arthur supplied. Out of love for his daughter the knight dispatched two pack horses, heavily laden with silver and gold, so that Koralus could get fine clothing and equipment for the journey to Destrigales, the land of Erec's father. He also sent a messenger to King Lac to ask that his old father-in-law be given two castles in his land to rule as his own and suggested those of Montrevel and Roadan. His request was granted. When the noble man took possession of them, he was compensated for all the hardships he had suffered. Not only was he relieved of want, but he became so rich that he could live in the splendid manner suitable to his high rank.

[1838] Let us now return to our story. After Erec had arrived at the court and the king had taken his reward, the beauty and kindness of Lady Enite, who looked like an angel as she sat there, filled Erec's heart with ardent desire. To wait for her love any longer than until the coming night seemed to him much too long. Since Enite's secret wish was the same as his, they probably would have begun a most loving game if no one had been watching. I tell you truly, Dame Love was the victor here: she ruled them and caused them great distress.

[1861] Looking at each other, they felt not unlike a hungry falcon that chances to catch sight of its meal. Although at other times it may have gone longer without eating, it is much hungrier once it has been shown the food. In like measure and even more they were tormented by having to wait. Each thought, "I shall never be happy until I have lain two or three nights with you." They longed for love as a lonely child yearns for the mother who speaks kindly, always gives it good things, and wards off with her hands whatever might harm it. Their desire was different—which is natural—but not less, and it was later satisfied.

[1887] The wedding day at last drew near, to the joy of both. The courtly Arthur insisted that Erec be married in Cardigan Castle so that his land might celebrate the occasion, and at once sent letters and messages everywhere, inviting the princes— and all others, far and wide, who heard the news—to come to the festival. The marriage was to take place at Whitsuntide.

[1902] I shall now give you the names of all the counts and the many ruling princes who attended the festival at which Erec married Enite. They were great lords: Count Brandes of Doleceste, who brought a retinue of five hundred men (all finely equipped and dressed in his colors); Count Margon of Glufion; the lords of Haute Montagne, near Britain; Count Libers of Treverin, with a hundred companions; the mighty Count Grundregoas; Sir Maheloas of Crystal Island, whose land was most pleasant—as everyone knows—with neither vermin nor storms, nor weather too hot or too cold; Gresmurs of Fine Posterne, whom all were glad to see; his brother Gimoers, lord of the Isle of Avalon, on whom fortune smiled because of his love for a fairy named Marguel; Davit of Luntaguel; and Duke Guelguezins of Haut Bois, who arrived with a splendid company of retainers.

[1939] You have heard the list of dukes and counts, now learn also of the kings who came. There were ten, so they say: five young and five old, all rich and powerful. They had joined each other in knightly fashion to form two groups, the young and the old, as was fitting. It is said that the younger ones were dressed and mounted alike, as were the older, and in a manner suitable to their station. I'll describe the robes of the former for you. They were of various colors of samite and silk interwoven with gold, cut to fit—neither too narrow nor too wide—and lined with many-colored fur. Their horses were black as ravens and always moved at a trot. The young kings entered the land first, each with a four-year-old sparrow hawk on his hand. It was a splendid company, for all had retinues of three hundred well-dressed men. There were King Carniz of Schorces, King Angwisiez of Scotland with his two sons Coin and Goasilroet, and King Beals of Gomoret.

[1978] After these young knights the five mighty old kings arrived in majesty. They too had similar clothing and mounts. It is said that they had donned robes in keeping with their age—made of the best fine, dark cloth to be found in all England, with linings of a gray fur which could not be surpassed anywhere, not even in Russia or Poland. They were long and wide, with small plates of thick gold leaf all around: the workmanship was so elegant, beautiful, and artistic that one ought to praise it at length. At the hems were broad bands of sable—no better or more costly could be found in all Conneland. This is a large country which produces the world's best sable. It lies between the lands of the Greeks and the heathen and is ruled by the sultan.

[2012] Such were their robes. Underneath they wore furs that were just as costly, and each of their hats was of splendid sable. They were well mounted, as I shall tell you. Their palfreys were snow-white and adorned in keeping with the wealth of the old kings. The riding equipment glittered with fine gold, for all the metal parts were inlaid with silver and plated with gold and the saddle girths were broad bands of silk interwoven with gold.

[2029] When this troop rode into Britain, each of them held on his hand a beautiful peregrine falcon which was six years old or more. They were well entertained while traveling the three leagues to the castle, for the hunting was good. The lakes and ponds were covered with ducks, and all other prey of the falcon was found there in great numbers. Never before had falcons made so many successful flights. The kings saw ducks and wood grouse, herons and pheasants, cranes and wild geese fly up before them. Many bustards also hung from the saddles of their squires, because everything that was raised was caught. The fields were completely emptied of game: if a hare started up, it was his last race. When they rode on after the hunt, a friendly dispute broke out, for each maintained that his falcon had flown the best. This still happens today.

[2064] Leaving his castle, King Arthur now rode toward them and received the stately companies with great honor; he was very pleased that they had come. The noble knights were welcomed as their station required and treated even better. I'll tell you the names of the old kings. One was the wise and upright King Jernis of Riel, who brought with him a praiseworthy train of three hundred men. Hear how old they were. The hair of their heads and beards was white as snow and had grown so long that it reached their belts. Truly, the youngest was a hundred and forty years of age.

[2086] Now hear about the other kings. The dwarf King Bilei and his brother Brians, both of the land of Antipodes, were there. No sons of the same mother were ever more unlike. The true story tells us that Brians was taller by a span and a half than anyone else of his time in all the lands, and it is said that there was no dwarf then or even before who was shorter than Bilei. But what he lacked in size, the little stranger made up for in courage. Moreover, no one was his equal in wealth. He arrived in splendor with a large company and brought along two friends, Grigoras and Glecidolan, who were also rulers over dwarf lands. These were the kings. Arthur received the mighty guests at Cardigan with great honor.

[2118] The day had now come when Erec the son of King Lac was to wed Enite. Since both were happy at the prospect, why should they wait longer? The bishop of Canterbury in England married them, and a celebrated festival began; no poverty was seen there. So many noble knights were present that I have little to say about what they ate, because they were concerned with excelling in other ways than by gluttony. Therefore I'll speak only briefly of the feast: there was an abundance of all that from which men and horses live, and they were served without stint. However, they took only as much as was proper.

[2142] As soon as the meal was over, the bohort and the dancing began and lasted until night. Their joy became greater as every sorrow was forgotten. The knights went to greet the ladies, who received them cordially. Their spirits were gladdened by this welcome and also by the storytelling, the sweet stringed music, the singing, the lively dancing, and many other kinds of amusements. They could enjoy fine performances of every sort, for more than three thousand of the best minstrels in the world—masters of their arts—were present. There never was a more splendid festival before or since.

[2166] Not one of those people who entertain for pay was turned away. Such wanderers have a certain habit: if one gets a lot and another doesn't, the latter is envious and spreads a bad report of the celebration. However, there were no quarrels here, because all were very well rewarded and became equally rich. Many a man who never before had gotten half a pound received thirty marks of gold. Minstrels probably will never again get so much. Both clothing and horses were given these lowly people about whom no one before had ever been concerned. Care was thus taken that no one became angry at another because of possessions, since everybody at once received enough and no one needed to feel ashamed. Moreover, the giving of presents did not cease for fourteen days, until the end of the festival.

[2195] This was the wedding of Erec the son of King Lac. When the celebration was over, many minstrels left happily, with full hands and singing its praises. With one accord they all spoke highly of the festivities and wished Erec and Enite every happiness—which indeed they were to enjoy for a long time. Their wish was fulfilled, for never did two people love each other more until they were parted by death, which comes between one love and another and turns all joy to sorrow. The princes too were about to say good-by when their host extended the festival by two more weeks. He did this for Erec, of whom he was very fond, and also for Enite. This second period of merrymaking was as joyous as the first, even more so.

[2222] Some began now to say that since they had come to Britain for entertainment, it was not proper for a brave man to leave without taking part in a tournament. Gawein at once replied that they should have one and challenged these four friends: Entreferich, Tenebroc, Meliz, and Meljadoc. It was arranged that the tournament should take place three weeks from the following Monday and was to be held—so the story goes—between Tarebron and Prurin, which was halfway from each of the two parties. The four men took their leave without delay in order to make preparations, because the time was short.

[2248] Since Erec had never taken part in a tournament, he

considered at length how he could attend in a manner befitting his rank. It often occurred to him that the reputation which a young man gets in his first years as a knight may easily remain with him for life, and he feared long-lasting disdain. He was therefore quite concerned about how to make a good impression. Erec was not rich enough to do everything he wished, but since he was a stranger and far from home, King Arthur gave him all he needed as soon as he asked. In keeping with his sense of propriety, the young man was considerate enough not to request too much and to evade the king's generosity with protests whenever he could. He would have done wonders if he had had all the means he wanted; however, he made his preparations in accordance with his present condition and made do with what he had. Had he been rich, both his armor and his attendants would have been finer.

[2285] Erec caused three shields and three sets of riding equipment to be adorned with the same coat of arms, although in different colors. One shield, which was very solidly built, shone as brightly and as far as a mirror on the outside and displayed a full-sized golden sleeve; on the inside it was gold. The second was bright red, and fastened to it was a gleaming silver sleeve of the best workmanship possible in such a short time. It was like the first on the inside and was very beautiful. The third was gold, outside and inside, and had a sable sleeve that could not have been finer. It was fastened to the shield by a clasp and by silver branches—neither too broad nor too narrow—which embraced the entire surface. On the upper part of the inner side was the picture of a lady; the strap, like those of the other two shields, was a silk and gold band with precious stones.

[2320] Erec now took care to have three banners quickly made, each to match a different shield. With King Arthur's help the young man also obtained helmets from Poitiers, hauberks from Schamliers, greaves from Glenis, and five horses from Spain. For each horse he procured ten gaily colored spears, the heads of which were made in Lofanige and the shafts in Etel-burg. His helmet was splendidly adorned with a shining angel that stood in a golden crown. Surcoat and caparison matched and were made of green samite and fine silk which were trim-

med with embroidered bands. He secured fifteen very able
squires—the equals of any in all Britain—and fitted them out
with splendid cuirasses and helmets; each carried a well-
trimmed staff.

[2351] While Erec was getting ready, a wagon carried his
spears to the place between Tarebron and Prurin, because the
time for the tournament was at hand and many noble knights
were arriving. When he said good-by to Enite, there was a fair
exchange between the two. I'll tell you of what kind: the faithful
man took her heart away with him and left his own behind,
locked up in the breast of the lady.

[2368] King Arthur rode up to the tournament grounds on
Saturday evening with all his troops, the noblest of whom were
lodged as usual close by. They amused themselves noisily in
knightly fashion, and all their tents were bright with candles
until dawn. Erec, however, chose a place at some distance from
the others and took no part in the celebrating. He passed the
time in seclusion like a prudent man, not wanting to act like a
great knight, which was wise.

[2386] Only those who, in contrast to him, had often before
competed in tournaments should indulge in such revelry. Erec
didn't think it could be permitted him, since he did not consider
himself experienced enough nor famous for bravery. But those
of his companions who were so friendly as to seek out his lodgings were received more cordially than at other places. Whatever else might have been lacking, his good will was so apparent
that each of them was glad for any opportunity to praise him. He
acted like a true child of Dame Fortune, which is why everyone
liked him and spoke well of him.

[2404] The knights enjoyed themselves, as is usual at tournaments. On Sunday they made their final preparations by
having their armor polished and provided with new straps:
there was nobody who was not a credit to the occasion. Erec put
on his armor before anyone else—it was barely noon—in order
to get ahead of the others and, if possible, take part in the first
joust. Two friends, brave knights who also had this in mind,
came onto the field at the same time as he and galloped confidently toward him as soon as they saw him. In the jousts that
followed, Erec struck first one and then the other to the ground,

but did not bother to take possession of their horses because he wanted to seek out further contests.

[2433] He then jousted five more times with great skill, which brought him honor and praise. Two things helped him, good luck and the exceptional natural ability that God had given him. The jousts took place very early, before the main body of knights had arrived at the field; however, now—to Erec's renown—they rode up from all sides and saw the riderless horses running about. "Good God," they all cried, "who turned these horses loose? It must have been Erec."

[2453] A large number of knights at once began a preliminary tournament, which became a hard-fought contest because the two sides were equal in strength. There were fine individual jousts, mass charges of one troop into another, and swordplay. Erec was in constant motion: anyone watching him could not let his eyes rest, for he was everywhere. No knight ever competed better than he, and each onlooker was gazing at him alone; he was always the first to enter a fray and the last to leave it. Both sides praised him without a dissenting voice. He rode until night intervened. When they went to their lodgings, one could hear nothing but "Erec the son of King Lac is the best man for his age that our country has had. He could not conduct himself better." This was the general opinion. The contest before the tournament earned him renown.

[2487] Erec was up early the next morning. Before doing anything else, he went to church—as a knight should—and commended himself to the one whose mercy never fails, who has never withheld aid from an upright man. He who looks to God in all things can expect to succeed, and Erec fully trusted him to care for his knightly honor. As soon as the benediction was given, he had his shield and horse brought to him and rode onto the field with neither armor nor companions—except for his five squires—which, it seems to me, is proof of his great and praiseworthy courage. Each squire carried three spears that he used up in real jousts, although bare of armor, without any of his party knowing it. After this success he stole back to them and acted as if nothing had happened.

[2516] However, early in the morning Dame Gossip had sent a page to the field to see what honor and fame Erec had won. The chatterbox told King Arthur and then began to reprove the knights who were still in bed and scold them for being asleep. "Why are you lying here?" he said. "Who ever gained honor by sleeping? Erec has already done great feats with spear and sword today. May God grant him good luck whenever he asks for it. I shall always praise him because I have seen him perform great deeds that will make him famous for all time." Erec thus gained still more friends and became even more highly regarded than before.

[2538] He had only a short rest, for as soon as he entered his lodgings the other knights left theirs and went to mass, as those should do who intend to compete in a tournament. He had a little to eat and drink, but his desire to return to the field kept him from taking much. It was surprising how quickly all now donned their armor; he did the same. They had barely finished when they saw the four companions—Entreferich, Tenebroc, Meliz, and Meljadoc—riding across the arena with their standards. Behind them came a powerful force of bold knights and many more fine banners of different colors. Erec and Gawein and the rest of the knights of their company rode forth at once, and loud battle cries arose in front of the banners.

[2566] Erec began the attack in a knightly manner. His surcoat and crown were so splendid that he could be recognized farther than anyone else. When he was near enough to the opposing party for a joust, a brave man, the proud Lando, restrained his companions from attacking and rode toward him. The knight had triumphed so often before that he was considered the best in his country, but Erec nevertheless succeeded in knocking him from his horse. He then further distinguished himself by using up twelve more spears between the two companies, while his great ability kept him from being harmed.

[2589] He kept on until his shield was so badly broken and cut by spears and swords that it was worthless. Then he rode away, as carefully as he could, and exchanged shield, horse, and banner for new ones. Before Erec returned, however, his entire company attacked, and he was no longer able to joust between the two forces. There was now fierce fighting with spears and swords everywhere, and many spears were shattered as the knights on both sides eagerly charged at each other. The noise of

the breaking spear shafts could be compared only to the sound of
a mighty wind tearing down a forest. Erec outdid all the rest in
the number of saddles emptied on this Monday, but he let the
horses run and took none of them, for he had not come to gain
booty. His mind was set only on winning the greatest fame: I can
tell you truly that he did not spare himself. Now that the conflict
had become general, he was usually seen in the very middle of it,
fighting bravely, dealing out and receiving blows.

[2630] After Erec had wielded spear and sword until he was
tired, he withdrew to rest a bit. When he dismounted, a merce-
nary took his horse, thanking him warmly for it. He untied his
helmet, and his squires were there at once to loosen his cap so
that he could cool off. However, he had no chance to do so and got
only a short rest, because just then he saw his companions
slowly retreating, pushed back step by step, and was afraid that
they were close to defeat. He sprang on his horse so hastily that
he forgot his helmet and sat there bareheaded: it was just luck
that he happened to seize his shield and spear. He didn't wait
then, but, with banner streaming, made a splendid charge.

[2657] If Erec had not come quickly to the aid of his company,
it would have suffered severe losses and been vanquished. This
was clear since the entire force had ceased fighting and pulled
back except only three: the noble Sir Gawein, who excelled in
every way and had never been defeated, with Duke Gilules's son
and Segremors at his side. These knights held firm against the
opposing troops. Never had three men fought better, I assure
you: neither spear thrusts nor sword blows could move them
from their place. Still, they would have been taken prisoner
because of their adversaries' superior force—the lord of all
things, against which one can do nothing—if Erec had not ridden to them in their need, as a friend should, dashing up like a
roaring wind. He was so valiant that he soon drove them all
back.

[2688] Once more he had to struggle fiercely; otherwise it
would have turned out differently. The noble Boidurant jousted
against him but was unhorsed with a spear thrust, for which
Erec won praise. In a short time he had driven the enemy back a
third of a league all by himself. Seeing this, his companions
turned around and came to his aid in full force, pushing the

unresisting adversaries right up to the boundary of the field.

[2704] Erec then gave away the third horse. His company had gained a splendid victory, which without him would not have been possible, and many of his comrades won a large amount of booty because of him. They thanked him for this and found it all the more fitting to sing his praises. They considered it a great deed that Erec, although his head was bare, did not let his vulnerable condition keep him from riding to them and bravely driving the enemy back.

[2720] Gawein did well that day, as on other occasions and as was his custom. It was the usual thing with him, so they say, that whatever knightly deeds he chanced to perform, no one could maintain that another had done them better. For this reason he is still famous. He had a most knightly spirit, was rich and noble, had only good qualities, and hated no one. He was loyal, generous without regrets, stable and well-mannered, truthful, strong, handsome, and brave. He was lighthearted, charming, and possessed a wealth of every virtue. Perfection itself had fashioned him, and in such a manner—of this we have been assured—that no other knight so faultless had ever appeared at Arthur's court.

[2745] What an excellent vassal Gawein was for the king! He was willing to suffer for honor's sake and showed great courage that day, winning both goods and fame: early in the contest he captured two knights, Ginses and Gaudin de Montein. Only Erec had more success, and I would rate him higher for this one day. However, I wouldn't dare do so for a longer period because it is said that the like of Gawein never came to Britain. But if his equal nevertheless did appear there, it must have been Erec. The youth's many virtues make this clear.

[2764] When the enemy was driven to the boundary, Erec asked whether anyone wished to come forward and joust for the honor of his lady. A knight named Roiderodes at once replied that he would be glad to joust if it could be done without enmity or forfeits. Very pleased, Erec agreed and charged. As he had often proven already, he was fearless. The two dashed eagerly at one another, and each soon used up twelve spears without a single miss. Then Erec got off his horse, gave it away, and mounted the fifth one, which stood ready for him. He was determined to end the matter—and soon did—for he didn't want to keep his friends waiting any longer. He asked that the course be cleared and took his spear under his arm. Then the two rode boldly at each other. This time Erec struck squarely on the four nails of his opponent's shield with such force that the breastplate, girth, and surcingle of the knight's saddle all parted like rotten bast, leaving only the broken reins in his hands: he fell at least three spear-lengths from his horse. Erec kept his seat and won praise and honor thereby.

[2807] There was nothing more to be done; the tournament ended and King Arthur's retinue left the field as victors. Erec received in full measure the praise he deserved. He was compared to Solomon in wisdom, to Absalom in beauty, and to Sampson in strength, and he seemed so liberal that they could liken him in this respect only to the generous Alexander. Erec's shield was badly broken and had holes from spear thrusts that one could put a fist through: he had earned his acclaim.

[2826] When the story spread and Lady Enite heard of her husband's great feats, his bravery brought her both joy and pain. She was happy because they spoke well of him and sad because she could see his spirit was such that, unless God in mercy protected him, she would not have him long, for he would readily risk his life for honor whenever he sought it, whereas a timid man would not care whether he was praised or condemned. But quickly deciding that she would rather have a warrior than a worthless coward for a husband, she ceased her petty lamenting and was happy and proud of his bravery.

[2852] As soon as the tournament was over, the king and his retinue rode back to Cardigan, where each lady, including Enite, received her knight joyfully. She and Erec did not stay much longer at the court. He asked King Arthur for leave to go in order to return home to Destrigales, his father's land. It seemed to him high time, because he had not been there since childhood. When would be better than now? Having resolved to go, Erec chose sixty companions, whom he equipped well and dressed like himself, and took them along for company. He sent a courier on ahead to tell his father that he was coming.

[2881] The man hurried at once to Karnant (the capitol of the country), found the king there, and delivered his son's message.

This earned the courier a rich gift, for the king never had a happier day than when he heard that his dear son was returning to him: he was delighted. He quickly sent for his relatives and vassals, of whom he mustered over five hundred, and all rode for three days to meet Erec. According to the story, they received the knight and his wife in a very friendly manner: indeed, no lady was ever greeted more warmly than she was then.

[2904] The old King Lac was delighted, because both Erec and Enite were a feast for his eyes; whether he looked to the right or to the left, he was happy: the one was very handsome and the other was beautiful. He was pleased with his son—as a father should be when his child is so good-looking and praiseworthy—but even more with Enite. As soon as he brought them home to Karnant, he showed them his satisfaction by putting the two in charge of the country, Erec as king and Enite as queen. He turned over all the power to them.

CHAPTER 2

Alienation

[2924] Erec was upright and capable, and, before marrying and returning home, had had a knightly spirit. Now, however, he thought only of Enite's love and was concerned simply with arranging everything for their comfort. His habits changed, and he passed the days as if he had never been a brave warrior. Mornings he lay in bed and caressed his wife until the bell rang for mass. Then they got up quickly, went hand in hand to the chapel, and left just as soon as the service was over. This was his greatest exertion. By now the meal was ready. After they finished eating, Erec and his wife left the others and fled to their bed, where the lovemaking was resumed. He did not appear again until the evening meal. However, when Erec gave up knightly pursuits, he kept one virtue for which I praise him: he provided so well for all his men that they could afford to go to tournaments even though he did not. He ordered that they be as finely equipped as if he were riding with them.

[2966] Erec turned to a life of ease because of his wife, whom he loved with such passion that, to be with her, he gave up all striving for honor and became indolent to the point where no one could respect him. The knights and squires at the court were rightly annoyed at this. Those who before had led a merry life there now became very bored and left, because no one doubted that he had become quite worthless: this was his repute. A change had taken place in Erec so that his former fame had become shame and everyone spoke scornfully of him. His court was joyless and fell into decay; there was no need to come from foreign lands to seek pleasure here. Those who were subject to

64

him and wished him well then began to speak bitterly and say, "Cursed be the hour when we first saw our lady, for our lord is going to ruin because of her."

[2999] This talk spread until it got to Enite. She was deeply troubled on hearing the reproaches, because she was fine and noble, and she tried to think of some way to appease the enmity which everyone felt toward her. Aware that it was her fault, she bore the sorrow in a womanly manner and did not dare say anything to Erec for fear of losing him.

[3013] Once Erec was lying in her arms at midday as usual, and the sun, wishing to serve the two lovers, shone through a window and filled the room with light so that they could see each other clearly. Then Enite chanced to think of the curses which had been directed at her and abruptly moved from Erec. She looked at him earnestly and, believing him asleep, sighed deeply. "Alas for you, poor man," she said, "and for me, wretched woman, that I should hear so many condemn me."

[3033] Erec heard her plainly and, when she was silent, spoke up, "Enite, tell me what are these sorrows which you lament in secret?" She tried to deny that she had any, but he replied, "Stop that! Just keep in mind that I intend to know what you were talking about. You must tell me what it is that I heard you bewailing and that you have been keeping from me." Since she was afraid of being accused of other offenses, she told him, under the condition that he promise not to be angry.

[3050] When he learned what the trouble was, Erec said, "I've heard enough," and at once bade her get up and put on her best clothing. He then told his squires to get his horse and Enite's palfrey ready, asserting that he wanted to go for ride. While they hurried to do his will, Erec secretly dressed himself in armor and put on his clothing over it. He then tied on his helmet without first donning a protective cap. Since he was determined to conceal his intentions, he resorted to a clever ruse. "My helmet is not right," he said. "I am glad that I noticed. If I had needed it, I would have been in an awkward situation. I'll tell you what is wrong: it needs new straps."

[3077] No one could have guessed what he had in mind. He took shield and spear from the wall and gave a battle cry as if he were going to a tournament. But when his knights and squires started to ride off with him, he told them to remain there and sent word to the kitchen that the cooks should take care to have the meal ready for them as soon as they returned. Having given these instructions, Erec went off with the beautiful Enite. He ordered her on pain of death to ride in front and never say a word during the journey, no matter what she saw or heard. She was frightened by this threat and promised to obey his strange command.

[3106] The two rode through fields and woods until dark. Night fell and the bright moon shone as the brave warrior continued on in search of knightly adventure. The road led them into a thick forest that was controlled by three robbers who watched the road and, in order to seize his possessions, took life and honor from anyone who came their way at that time without a strong escort. Since Enite was some distance ahead, she saw them before Erec did. For the first time on the journey she was greatly distressed, because she could tell by their actions that they were robbers. She tried to let Erec know with signs, but he had not seen them himself and could not understand her, which almost was his undoing.

[3134] Enite then was sorely troubled, for she saw the danger and was afraid of losing the dearest man a woman ever had: his situation was indeed perilous. What could compare with the bitter grief that her loyalty caused her to suffer because of her husband! As she rode on in despair, unable to decide whether to risk telling Erec or to keep silent, she thought, "Almighty and gracious God, in mercy help me: you alone know my plight. I am deeply troubled, for I am suddenly caught up in a frightful game and cannot see the best move. What will become of poor me? I shall lose, whichever course I choose. To warn my dear husband will cost me my life, but if I keep still, he will be killed. A woman's heart is too weak for so desperate a choice."

[3167] She then made up her mind. "It would be better that I die," she thought, "whom no one needs lament, than such an excellent man whose death would be a great loss for many. He is noble and powerful, and we are not of like value. I shall die rather than see him perish. Whatever happens to me, my husband shall not lose his life as long as I can prevent it." Enite therefore looked around fearfully and said, "Look up, my dear lord. Permit me to tell you in loyalty—for I can't be silent when danger threatens you—that there are knights nearby who will harm you if they can, if God doesn't protect you." Erec prepared to fight.

[3190] Meanwhile one robber, the first to see them, said to his companions: "I have good news which will improve our fortunes. Over there I see a man riding who, as well as I can make out at this distance, is escorting a woman. You can easily tell by their fine equipment and splendid clothing that they are rich. Our poverty is ended, for I think they will have much wealth with them. I want to remind you lords now to keep the bargain we made: you are to grant me the first choice with this booty and also the first joust with yonder knight because I was the first to see them. If I kill him, I'll take only the woman; that's all I want of his property." They agreed that he should have this honor.

[3216] When Erec came near, the robber raised his shield, spurred his horse, and cried: "Sir, you have lost your property and your life." Too angry to reply, the knight struck him down from the horse dead. His companions tried to avenge him and suffered the same fate. Erec's victory was partly due to the fact that their arms and legs were unprotected. As is usual with robbers, they were lightly armed, wearing only helmet and cuirass. The knight made use of this weakness and quickly cut them down, one right after the other.

[3225] As soon as Erec's courage had brought the struggle to a happy end, he spoke to Enite: "How is this, strange woman? I forbade you to speak on pain of death. Who told you to ignore my order? I have found out here that what I had heard about women is true, that whatever was strictly forbidden them is just that which they had an urgent longing to try. It is a waste of time to tell you not to do something, because this only entices you until you can't abstain. You therefore deserve scorn. What a woman would never think of doing if it were permitted, she will do at once as soon as it is forbidden: she simply can't resist then."

[3259] "My lord," replied Enite, "I would not have done it if I had not been concerned about your safety. I spoke only out of loyalty. If you think that I was wrong, then forgive me for your honor's sake. It won't happen again."

"See that it doesn't," said Erec. "I'll let it go unpunished, but I shall not spare you a second time. Still, you will not profit by this disobedience because you must atone for it in part. You shall have the horses fully in your keeping and shall care for them well. You are to serve as my squire."

[3277] "So be it, my lord," answered the noble Enite and was not offended. In a most womanly manner she endured the unfamiliar work, together with all else that grieved her heart, without complaint. Seizing their reins, she took charge of the horses and rode ahead, as Erec had commanded. She managed the horses as well as a lady could: she couldn't do any better.

[3291] Not long afterwards—they had ridden only three leagues—she again became alarmed, because she saw five robbers lying in wait before her. It is said that there was an agreement between them and the ones Erec had killed by which they shared the plunder and kept each other posted. These five and those three controlled the forest and lurked by the road, so that whoever avoided one group would ride into the hands of the other. As you have heard, Erec came away from the three with honor. When he now approached the five, one of them—who was stationed at some distance from the others as a sentinel—caught sight of him and was pleased.

[3317] "Here is good news," he reported back to his companions. "We shall all be rich. I have seen people coming whom we can easily defeat, for there seems to be only one man. With him is a noble lady who is leading three horses. It is hard for her, and it looks to me as if she were not suited for this task. I wonder where he got such an unusual squire. It is only right that we should take her away from him. From this distance she appears to be the most beautiful woman I have ever seen. You lords must leave her to me, because I saw her first." They all agreed that his claim was just.

[3338] "Hear what part of the booty I want," spoke a companion of the sentinel; "only the knight's armor, nothing more." The others then divided up the five horses. It was unkind to assign the armor, which was supposed to serve Erec himself, who needed it. But nothing came of the allotment.

[3348] Erec, who didn't know what had been said, now came into the view of the band, and one of them prepared to attack him. This caused Enite great concern. "If I warn my husband," she thought, "I shall be defying his order again, and he will not spare me either for honor's sake or for God's sake. What an unlucky woman I am! I would rather be dead than in such dreadful straits: I would be far better off. If I should just look on and see the man killed who raised me from poverty to be mistress of such great wealth that I am honored and known as a mighty queen, I would bitterly regret it, for then my soul would be lost and rightfully die with my body. May God show me, poor woman, what to do so that in my haste I don't make a mistake. Should I keep still? No, certainly not, I must tell him. Whatever the danger to me, I shall risk it as before."

[3378] She turned around quickly and spoke fearfully to Erec: "My lord, for God's sake hear me! Watch out or you will be slain. I see five companions who intend to kill you." As soon as he heard this, Erec got ready to fight.

One of the robbers left the others and, unfortunately for him, rode ahead to joust with the knight; a thrust of Erec's spear and he lay dead under his horse. There were still four left. The knight quickly struck another dead from his mount but broke his spear doing so and had to put his sword to work. However, it was not long until he felled the other three and they were lying on the ground with their comrades.

[3400] When the one man had thus defeated five and was about to ride on, he spoke to Enite: "Tell me, defiant woman, why did you break your word again? Wasn't it enough that I put up with it once without your doing it another time? If a knight could gain honor by fighting a woman, this would be no trifling matter for you, because I would kill you here and now."

[3413] "Have mercy, lord," she answered. "You should consider that I did it because I was loyal. Whatever happens to me, I would rather suffer your anger than have you die. If I had waited longer, you would have been killed. I shall gladly keep silent from now on. Just forgive me for God's sake, and if I disobey you any more, you can punish me on the spot."

[3425] "Let me tell you, lady," said Erec, "you will get nothing but trouble from this stubbornness. You will pay for it. Your punishment will be the same as before: I will use you as a squire throughout the journey. Now take charge of the horses and keep them well or your wages will be most unpleasant. Should one of them become lost, you will see some wrath that, if you are wise, you would be glad to do without."

[3440] Enite gathered the horses together. Where before there were three, there now were eight. She led them as best she could, but did not manage very well. Yet, although such labor was by no means customary for ladies and was an affront to her station, her kindness enabled her to endure it cheerfully and without complaint. Enite would have suffered sore distress if she had not changed the sorrow to joy in her heart. Humility taught her that. Who considers the matter will agree that it would have kept four squires busy to lead and care for eight horses properly, which she had to do by herself. If Dame Fortune had not stood by my lady and God's courtesy had not hovered over her to prevent any great mishap with the beasts, her journey would have been troublesome indeed. However, she was well protected against this. Moreover, with such a keeper, they could not help but curb their wild willfulness and go along gently.

[3472] They rode quickly out of the forest just at the dawn of a fine day. When it became lighter, Erec saw that the road ahead led to a nearby castle where the lord of the country, a mighty count, lived. Since they had endured hardships and ridden all night without food, both were pleased at the sight, because they thought they could rest a day in the small market town below the castle. They were hurrying toward the town when they met a youth who was carrying boiled ham and bread, carefully wrapped in a white towel (as he had been ordered), and a jug of wine.

[3499] As the youth rode toward the two, he looked closely at the harried woman and was surprised at the number of her charges. She greeted him in a friendly manner when he came abreast of her, and he thanked her with a bow as he continued on his way. Then he came to Erec, who wished him a good morning from under his helmet. He could easily see that the knight had ridden in armor all night and had had a difficult time.

[3514] Moved by their troubles, the youth spoke: "Sir, if you won't take it amiss, I would like to ask where you are going. Be so kind as to tell me, for I have only the best intentions. I have always lived in this country and am a squire of the count, while you seem to be a stranger here. I beg you most cordially to honor my lord by going to his castle to rest from your toilsome journey. This appears fitting, and I beg you for God's sake to do it, because they will be happy to serve you there. You look as if you had ridden long and suffered hardships: I have ham, bread, and very good wine with me should you be hungry. Now do me the favor of asking the lady to come, and you can eat right here."

[3541] Erec did as he was requested, which pleased the squire, who then hurried to Enite to take the horses from her. While she was going back to her companion, he tied the horses together. After that he removed his cloak, went hat in hand to get some water, and brought enough for the two to wash their hands. The squire then spread the towel on the grass and placed on it the food: meat, bread, and wine. There was nothing else.

[3556] When they had had enough to eat and had mounted their horses, Erec spoke to the squire: "Friend, it is right that you should receive a return for your kindness, because you have well earned our affection. Since I have neither silver nor gold with which to pay you, do as I ask and choose the horse which pleases you most. If the time ever comes when I can reward you better, you may be sure that I shall not refuse to do so. Please take the horse as a favor to us." The youth accepted one gladly. Erec would have given them all to him, but this would have made things easier for Enite. He kept the rest just to burden her.

[3580] When the youth had chosen the horse that best suited him, he thanked the knight warmly and said, "Dear sir, now grant my request and you will do me a great kindness. The labor of managing these horses causes the lady much distress. Permit me to lead them: I would enjoy it."

"You will have to forgo that, youth," replied Erec. "It can't be done without good reason, for she must endure hardships at this time."

"I shall leave you then," said the youth.

"Ride on and God go with you. May he repay you for your kindness and your gift—and guard your honor so that your life may be blessed."

[3600] Pleased with his own gift, the youth galloped joyfully off in the direction from which he had come: Erec rode slowly after him. The count, who had come out of the castle and was sitting in front of the gate, saw and recognized his squire from afar and was surprised that he was returning so soon. Later, when he asked whose horse he was leading, the youth quickly told him about his experience and added, "Look, sir, they are coming this way. Why are you waiting here instead of going down to the road to meet them? It would be unseemly not to, for you should give them a cordial welcome. You will find the lady to be the most beautiful woman either of us has ever seen."

[3624] The lord then went to the road and received Erec with a friendly greeting. As they rode up, he walked toward them, saying, "Welcome, lady and lord," and urged them to honor him by stopping over at his castle.

"Sir, you must excuse us," replied the knight. "The long journey has made us unpresentable and very tired. We thank you for your kind invitation, but permit us to decline it. For the time being allow us to ride on to an inn." They insisted until the count had to let them go; however, he asked a squire to lead them to the best inn in the town. Once there, Erec removed his armor while Enite turned over the horses to someone else and was happy to be able to rest. She felt like a soul which the archangel Michael has rescued from long suffering in the fires of hell. Erec ordered a bath—for he had become sweaty because of his exertions during the journey and was covered with rust from his armor—and washed himself clean. By the time his wife too had bathed, their meal was ready. When he was told of this, Erec had the table set, but he did not let Enite eat with him; he sat alone at one end and she alone at the other.

[3668] Meanwhile the count began to regret that he had been so upright as to let the woman go instead of having her seized for himself and, constrained by her beauty, began to consider how he might obtain her: treachery prompted him to make plans for taking her away from Erec. However, it was contrary to law and justice that he should try to seize the wife of a brave knight whom he ought to protect as a guest in his land if anyone wanted to harm him.

[3684] Love was to blame for his state of mind, because we have heard that the count had been a decent and kind man of honor up to this time. Mighty Love now robbed him of his reason and taught him treachery. With Love's snare one can often catch a man too clever to be trapped otherwise. The world has many

men who would never be misled to an evil deed were it not for
Love. If she did not exalt the spirit, one could make the world
better by doing away with her, for no one is strong enough to
escape Love once she has gained control of him. However, Love
will reward and never abandon the man who serves her faith-
fully in the right way, so that he will never have cause to regret
his devotion, provided that he guards his integrity better than
the count did. He was not steadfast in this, so Dame Love could
urge on him an evil thought and make him determined to take
the noble man's wife from him.

[3722] The count brought four knights with him to the inn and
found Erec and Enite at the table. He took off his mantle and
approached them with a greeting: Erec had no idea that he
wanted to harm him. The count was very surprised that the two
should sit far apart instead of together and said slyly: "Sir, if you
don't mind, I would like to know the reason for this. Is the lady
your wife? She is so pleasing and beautiful that it would be more
fitting for her to sit beside you than over there. Why did you
have her sit apart from you?"

[3745] "Sir," answered Erec, "that is simply my desire." When
the count then asked if he would object to his sitting with her
while they ate, the knight replied, "If you wish to, sir, I am
agreeable."

The count sat down beside Enite and said, "I'll tell you, lady,
why I came to you. It was partly for your material profit, but
mainly for your honor's sake. I was never so sorry for anyone as
for you, fair lady, when I saw you today enduring such unseemly
toil, which was never fitting for a lady. My heart was touched
and still pains me. I do not disdain you because of your great
poverty but am moved to pity, because truly you would be a
suitable wife for the emperor. Poor thing, who gave you to a man
like this one, who has neither the means nor the understanding
to honor you as you deserve? May God destroy this companion of
yours who uses you as a squire and is concerned only with
causing you grief.

[3778] "If God had granted you to me, you would be considered
worthy of much greater honors, but, should you wish it, everything good may still be yours. Lady, I'll let you know my will,
which you would be wise not to oppose, because I shall put an

end to your trouble. I'll tell you how things are with me. I am
lord of this land and truly have not been able to find a lady
anywhere who would suit me for a wife. However, you please me
so well that I would gladly make you mistress of my country.
Your condition would thus be much improved."

[3797] "For God's sake give up this plan," replied the noble
lady, "You would soon regret it, and rightly so, and I would seem
unfaithful. We would be objects of ridicule when everyone found
out about it! May God give you a wife who is more suitable for
you and your land. You can do better, because I am not fit to be a
countess: I am neither rich nor highborn. It is my duty to endure
whatever treatment I get from my husband, and I shall be fully
subject to him whether he wants me for a wife, a squire, or
anything else. Sir, why should I say more? For I would rather be
burned alive here and now and have my ashes scattered to the
winds than do as you suggest. My husband and I are suited to
each other. We are of like station, and neither of us is wealthy.
May God preserve him for me!"

[3826] When he heard this answer and learned how she felt,
the count spoke: "Listen to my intentions and judge by them
what action you should take. If you do not accede willingly to my
request, then you must do so unwillingly, for you cannot defend
yourself here. Your companion may go where he wishes, but you
shall stay with me. And that is that."

[3838] Seeing that he meant it, Enite looked at the treacherous man in a most friendly manner and laughed with fine guile.
"I believe you are in earnest," she said. "Sir, don't be angry at
me, since it is not necessary. I truly thought you were only
joking, because you men are accustomed to mislead—not to say,
deceive—us poor women by making great promises which you
do not expect to keep. I have often seen women suffer much grief
because of it. If I had not been afraid of this, my lord, I would
have given you a kinder answer, for I am not so foolish that I
would not improve my position by gaining honor and comfort.

[3863] "As you have seen, my life is quite wretched. I'll tell
you just how my husband got me for his wife, because we are not
of like station. He stole me away from my father, who in truth is
noble and wealthy. He often rode into our court, where I ran
about with others as children do. One day he played with us, and

it then became clear how easily children are deceived. He tricked me into going out of the gate with him, pulled me up onto his horse, bore me away, and has kept me like this ever since. I have had many wretched days because of him, for he dares not return to his own country, and I, unhappy creature, must always endure hardships and shame. If a man of nobler birth were to free me from this life and treat me honorably, I would gladly follow him and would pray God to reward him. I fancied you were speaking in jest, but if you promise me that you meant what you said, I am ready to do as you wish."

[3896] The count was pleased with these words and, smiling, answered her thus: "You cannot resist any longer then, since I shall swear to be true to you." Raising his fingers, he repeated the oath that the lady phrased. Thereupon she promised to do his will and laid her hand in his as a pledge, which proved to be unreliable.

After the agreement was made, Enite spoke with guile: "Sir, I advise you as one friend to another—for no man has my good wishes as you do—to follow my counsel: it won't cause you any trouble. Since you want to take me away, I suggest that you wait until tomorrow morning, when you can easily seize me without a struggle. Come while he is still in bed. He won't be able to harm you, because I shall steal his sword during the night. You will thus get me with no resistance. I love you now, for you well deserve it," she added, "and I am concerned that you may suffer injury because of me, which will surely happen if you do not do as I advise. Our relations are such that he won't be willing to let me go if you take me at this time. He has his sword at his side and, I know very well, will do some harm."

[3937] "It is good advice," replied the count, "and suits me so well that I shall gladly do as you say." Enite, a faithful wife, thus saved her honor and her husband's life with subtle woman's guile. She persuaded the man, and with false hopes, as I have said, he then took his leave.

As soon as they had finished eating, Erec had beds prepared for them in a bedroom; however, they were not to be next to each other, because he would not let Enite lie beside him. They then lay down to sleep, but not together: it was indeed strange that any anger could make him avoid such a beautiful woman.

Meanwhile, although driven by loyalty and kindness, she was sorely troubled about how her husband should learn of the count's plan, since he had forbidden her to speak no matter what she heard. She had not obeyed him—she would have lost him by doing so—and his anger at this made him unsociable, so that he ate and slept apart from her.

[3972] The noble lady was now thinking, "It has come to the point where the dearest husband a woman ever had will surely be taken from me if I do not warn him. Yet I know I shall suffer for it if I disregard his order again. Help me, mighty Lord God, for I was never so in need of your counsel! I know he will kill me, because he has spared me twice already. But what if I am slain: there still will be many good women alive. Moreover, there is no reason why I should be greatly mourned, while my dear lord is noble and rich. I would rather die than have anything harm him." Her faithful heart forced her, pale with fear, to go to his bed, kneel before him, and tell him the whole story.

[3998] As soon as Erec heard it, he got up, had the innkeeper awakened, and prepared to leave. He told the servants to get the horses ready, which was quickly done, and sent for the innkeeper. When the man came, Erec said, "You have treated us well here in your house and I owe you payment. Now listen to what it shall be. I have with me neither silver nor gold to give you, so do as I request and accept the seven horses as pay from me." The innkeeper bowed deeply, as a man does who gains much, and was very happy. At once he brought a cup so that the knight, for good luck on his journey, could drink St. Gertrude's love. Erec, the exile, thus rode off at night without delay and left the country with his wife, who had deceived the count with a pardonable lie.

[4028] Even before Erec set out, the traitor was thinking of how he would seize the lady when the time came to go to her. As he lay in bed he woke up in alarm, for he feared and believed that he was late. "To arms!" he cried loudly. "We have overslept. Up, you comrades who want to help me!" There were nineteen of them in all; he made twenty. After he had gathered his men, he went to the inn, called out fiercely, and kicked the door in. The innkeeper became alarmed and had begun to cry for help when the traitor said, "Can't you see who it is? Don't be afraid; just tell me what these lighted candles mean." They were the ones the brave Erec had left burning at his departure, but the count did not know that.

[4059] "Where are your guests sleeping?"

"They have gone, my lord."

"They haven't," spoke the count angrily.

"I would be foolish to lie, my lord."

"You are surely joking."

"No, sir, so help me God."

"You are. Lead me to them."

"Just have the place searched."

"I shall certainly do that."

"And I shall be glad to have you."

"How often must I ask you?"

"See for yourself where they were sleeping. Why shouldn't I tell you the truth about them?"

"I think you want to set me on the wrong track," said the count and acted as if he were about to kill him.

"Sir, God knows that they have gone."

"It is your fault."

"If you please, it truly is not."

"Otherwise they would have waited until daylight."

"Sir, they have just left."

"Tell me, have they gone far?"

"No indeed, my lord. They rode off only a short time ago."

"Where did they go?"

"I don't know."

[4084] The count's treachery now brought him deep sorrow, and he cursed his sleep fiercely. "Fate would not grant me honor," he said. "How could I have lost the most beautiful woman I ever saw anywhere only because of comfort! Cursed be the hour I went to sleep tonight!" Calling for the horses, he added, "Who arranges his affairs according to convenience, as I did tonight, ought to lose honor and win shame. Who ever gained something of value without effort? I got what I deserved." The count's squires then came riding up with the horses, and he delayed no longer. "Come on, you lords," he said. In their haste they had armed themselves only with shield and spear.

[4110] It was now light enough for them to see clearly the trail left by the horses' hoofs, and they followed it at a gallop. Meanwhile Erec had ridden some three leagues, since he was in a hurry to leave the country: through fear for his wife, not for himself. He knew that they would be pursued. When their rapid flight permitted him to say much, he spoke to Enite: "Lady, you have opposed me too stubbornly. I am very troubled because you persist in doing, and ever more freely, that which I forbade you on pain of death. I'll tell you my mind: I won't allow this, and it will really cost you your life if you do not stop it."

[4133] "Have mercy, my lord," she replied, "and consider that you would have been killed had I done otherwise. That is why it was best to disobey your order; however, I shall be careful never to do so again." But Enite now heard from afar the troop galloping furiously after them and, although she had just promised to give no further warnings, the vow was a fragile one which, compelled by the bonds of loyalty, she broke at once. "My dear lord," she said, "a large company is following you. They are riding so fast that I am sure they intend to harm you."

[4150] No one needs ask, How did it happen that the lady could both hear and see better than the knight? Because I shall tell you how it was. She was unarmed, while he, as is proper for a brave knight, was in full armor, which kept him from hearing and seeing as well as he could have without it. That is why a warning was necessary and saved him from death. His limited vision often would have cost him his life if his wife had not warned him, even though it made him angry.

[4166] Before Enite finished speaking, the count rode into view and, seeing Erec, called out in rude, unbridled fury with a hostile voice: "Look around, you worthless thief! Who could be pleased that you should lead a sweet and noble lady about in this land to the shame of us all? I tell you that I am going to kill you now. I would have you hanged right here if you were not a knight. You are holding her against the will of her family. Your riding off at night was a wretched trick, and one can guess by it that you stole her from her father. How else could you have gotten her? A fool could see that this lady is not suitable for you. If you want me to spare your life, vulgar thief, let her go. She won't have to live any longer in such misery, for I shall return her to her family. Now leave her and be on your way."

[4197] "You are forgetting all courtly manners," replied Erec. "Where did you learn to revile a knight this way? You were brought up in a boorish court. Shame on you for your lie: I am of more noble birth than you."

The combat began without further delay. They charged furiously at each other, and the deceitful man got the right pay for his treachery—a spear wound in the side that did not heal for a long time—because he was protected only by his shield. Also his arm was broken. When the count was struck from his horse, some loyal companions were very concerned and threw themselves over their lord to protect him. Others tried to avenge him at once with their swords, but they didn't hold out long. Erec killed six—they got enough fighting—and the rest, who were cowards, took flight even though no one pursued them. With that the conflict ended, and the knight, unharmed, rode hastily on his way.

[4232] "Merciful Lord God," he prayed, "protect me and help me to get out of the land without disgrace. If this becomes widely known, all the people will set out in pursuit at once and soon kill me." However, his anxiety was needless since no one heard of the matter until he was well out of the forest. He was very lucky. It was not reported because none of the surviving knights who remained with their lord wanted to leave him, and the cowards who fled kept silent from shame until Erec was far beyond the borders. The knights bound the wounds of the count and sadly brought him and the dead home on litters. This was the reward of his perfidy. When Erec was at last riding in a safe place where he did not have to fear the count, he scolded Enite for ignoring his order so often. He became frightfully angry, more furious than ever before, and she gave her word that she would never do this again, but she didn't keep it.

[4268] The perils Erec had endured thus far were of little account and child's play compared to that he was still to face, as I shall tell you. Both danger and sorrow were allotted to him, so he had much to suffer. The road now took him into a strange land whose ruler he did not know. Wondrous things have been told us of the latter's bravery. He was very small, if the report is true, and like a dwarf, except that his arms and legs were quite long. His chest was broad and thick, and in it beat a manly heart, which gave him his strength. That is what is important. Listen: if a man were twelve fathoms tall and had a weak and naturally timid heart, his great hulk would be useless. The case of this lord was different. One could tell a great deal about him, but that would make my story too long, so I shall shorten the account and leave much out.

[4304] The noble lord was high-spirited and lucky and had boldly defeated many men. It is therefore still said of him that his strength had never failed him until that day. The little man had conquered everyone, strong or weak, who fought against him. He never missed a tournament in his life which he was able to attend, and nobody there did better than he. [lacuna]

[4318] Enite once more showed her faithfulness to her husband when this new opponent appeared. After she had warned Erec, they watched him gallop up. He greeted Enite, and as soon as Erec had ridden within hearing distance, he said, "Welcome, sir. Whether you come to this land from far or near, I have no doubt but that you are a valiant warrior. This can be seen in two things. You are accompanying the most beautiful woman, on my soul, I ever met—who would have given her to a worthless fellow? Moreover, you are well armed, as befits a brave knight who is seeking adventure and does not want to be found defenseless at any time. God willing, you will get plenty of it here. I tell you truly, if you are lucky, you can win a victory now that will bring you much praise. Defend yourself, knight, it's time to begin."

[4348] "Brave and noble knight," answered Erec good-humoredly, "God forbid that you should do such injury to your good manners, for you would later regret it. You have just bid me welcome. How could you make up for your error if you were to fight me after that? It would be too rash and would not add to your fame. Since I have done nothing to you, leave me in peace for God's sake. I have ridden far and have endured such hardships that my whole heart is set against this."

[4366] "He is lamenting his troubles because he is afraid,"

thought the lord and said, "The fact that I welcomed you does not justify you in refusing, for I did so only in hope of a contest. And whatever I do now, you should not question my integrity, because I shall always preserve it. For the sake of your beautiful wife, defend yourself if you want to save your life."

[4378] When Erec saw that he would have to fight, he turned his horse around as his courage had taught him. Then the two men, neither of whom had ever known a trace of cowardice, charged at each other: strength and luck was to decide who was to be victor. The spears were thrust with such force that they splintered and the horses were thrown back on their haunches. The men therefore had to let go of the reins and attack each other in another fashion. They quickly dismounted and drew their swords. Each received here in full measure the favor for which he had long prayed: that God would send him a man on whom he could prove himself.

[4404] The knights began their fierce battle about noon. Fearing death and dishonor, Erec held his shield in front of him and skillfully protected himself without using his sword. The other did not guess his intention and cut away at the shield until nothing was left but the boss. Since there was no one on the heath to separate them, he then wounded Erec in the side: he thought the stranger was a coward. The beautiful Enite was in despair when blood poured from the wound and cried loudly, "Oh, my dear lord, if I could only take your place! I am afraid I have lost you."

[4434] "You are mistaken, lady," the undaunted man replied. "I would have to lose more blood than this." Thereupon he showed her the truth of his words. He no longer simply parried the blows of his opponent, but stepped forward a little and struck the little man so hard on the helmet that he fell wounded at Erec's feet. King Lac's son then almost committed an evil deed. He was about to kill the man when the latter cried out: "No, good knight! For the sake of your beautiful wife and your own noble spirit, honor God in me and let me live. I am willing to be subject to you. Allow me, who never before had a master, to be your vassal. If you had not won this honor through your bravery, I would rather die than let it happen, no matter how high your station might be. As it is, I do not care who your father may be, for your courage alone ennobles you so much that I shall be glad to have you for my lord."

[4460] Now the combat had lasted for nearly three hours, which seemed like a long summer day. When Erec gained the victory, he showed mercy to his opponent and spared his life. He helped him to his feet, untied his helmet, and said, "I ask only, and intend no affront, that you do me the honor of telling me your name. I want nothing more of you than to know who you are."

[4474] "Sir, it shall be as you wish: I shall tell you" was the reply. "I am king of Ireland and am called Guivreiz the Small." Erec did not take him as a vassal. Each lamented the other's injury, and Erec at once tore a strip from his surcoat—where could he find a better bandage at that time? Guivreiz tore one from his own, and each bound the other's wound, which he himself had made. This was most friendly. Enite, with her usual kindness, helped them. Afterwards they joined hands, pleased with each other, and sat down together on the grass, for they needed to rest. The fight had made them hot, and they were covered with blood and sweat. Enite sat down with them. She was both happy and sad, as I shall explain. She was happy at her husband's victory, but wept over his wound. The noble lady wiped the blood and sweat from them with the end of her wide sleeve.

[4509] As the two lords sat on the heath and cooled off, they talked as friends. "Sir," said the Irish king to the stranger, "do not take offense at what I am going to say, because it is only a whim. Your valor defeated me, and I was willing to be your vassal, which was a great success for you. I would be so even more gladly now if I could learn that your family is as noble as you have shown yourself to be. If you should tell me this, it would add to my honor. I was never overcome before, as I was by you, yet I shall feel fortunate—shall not lament but always be glad of it—if I was conquered by a highborn man."

[4535] "I'll tell you my family," answered the knight. "And I think it of noble lineage. My father is King Lac; my name is Erec." The king was pleased. As soon as he heard who the stranger was, he remained seated no longer but sprang up with joy, then fell at Erec's feet. "I shall gladly be your ever faithful vassal," he said, "and serve you in any way I can. I know your father well. Both I and my land shall be subject to you. Now you must reward my freely given oath of lifelong fealty by granting me a favor which I greatly desire of you. How could there ever be more faithfulness than that which two friends who trust each other owe one another? In the name of this loyalty I beg you as a favor to ride with me to my castle and remain there until you have recovered. Don't object. You will be doing me a kindness for which I shall always be indebted."

[4570] "I'll do as you ask," replied Erec, "if you won't expect me to remain so long. Don't be annoyed, but I can stay only until tomorrow morning. I'll tell you why: I am not traveling for pleasure and am indifferent to such comfort as I find, since I am not seeking it."

The king was pleased to have him as a guest. "Let us go," he said and walked toward the horses. With great courtesy he helped Enite into the saddle and rode on ahead with her while Erec followed. When they came up to the castle, his squires at once ran out from the gate to their lord and welcomed him with noisy rejoicing, for they all believed that he had captured this knight as he had many others. "It didn't turn out the way you think," he said and told them the full story of what had happened. "Those who are fond of me," he added, "should take care to give such a warm reception to the finest man I ever knew, that I may always reward them." They were glad to do so. Erec never received better care anywhere than he did that night.

[4614] While they were sitting together in the evening after having eaten, the host said, "Sir, I advise you to let us have a doctor treat our wounds. I think it would be dangerous for you to leave here now before you have healed. Unfortunately, you are seriously injured and, moreover, do not know the country. Things could easily go badly with you."

"Let us not talk about it," replied Erec, "for I can stay only until dawn." He was shown every honor that night as Guivreiz the Small did his best to see that his guest was given special attention until the next day.

CHAPTER 3

A Light Interlude

[4629,5] The good knight departed in the morning [lacuna] and, so we are told, entered a beautiful forest to which King Arthur with a splendid retinue had ridden from his castle at Tintajol, according to Chrétien, in order to hunt. Their camp was about a quarter of a league from the road. Sir Gawein came up at this time and tied his horse Wintwalite by his tent, where Keii found it. With Gawein's permission, he mounted it to go for a ride. He then picked up Gawein's shield and spear, which were nearby, and rode alone out to the road. There he caught sight of Erec, who was some distance off and riding toward him. When Keii could see him better, he noticed that the knight had ridden far, had suffered hardships along the way, and was stained with blood.

[4629,36] Getting an idea, Keii rode up to him, said deceitfully, "Welcome to this land, sir," and seized the bridle of his horse. He was afraid to attack the knight directly and thought that he could capture him in this manner. Keii asked who he was [lacuna] "You have no reason to be angry. I wanted you to go with me to where you can rest, for I see that you are badly wounded. My lord, King Arthur, is camped not far from here. I ask you in his name and that of the queen to ride there with me and recover from your troubles as their guest. They will be happy to see you." Here was his plan. Once he had brought the knight to the court, he would say that he, Keii, had wounded and captured him.

[4633] This clearly showed that the world has never known an odder person than him. There were four sides to his nature.

Sometimes it was adorned with great uprightness so that he regretted all the wrong he had done, was as free of falseness as a shining mirror, and avoided every evil word or deed. But his mood would change so that he soon forgot all decency. Then his only desire was to carry out zealously some deceit of word or deed, and nothing was bad enough to suit him. Moreover, on some days he was brave, on others very cowardly. These contrary traits harmed him in that he pleased no one and had a bad name everywhere. Because of his malice he was called Keii the Slanderer.

[4665] Now Erec could see very well what Keii had in mind and let him know it. "Sir," he said, "I have far to go and cannot ride out of the way at this time. If I were not in a hurry, I would travel a thousand leagues to be greeted by the king. Meanwhile, you must let me go my way. May God watch over you."

"Say no more, sir," replied the treacherous Keii, "because you shall not leave in this manner: it would not be proper for either of us. Truly, I intend to bring you to King Arthur's court if I am able." Erec became rather provoked and said, "I don't think you can, so it will be well for you if you are not in earnest. You will have to use force to get me there, but you can take me as a captive if you are brave enough."

[4694] "I know that I'm brave enough," answered Keii, "and sooner than let you dissuade me and ride off without seeing my lord, I'll force you to go, for your own good. You won't be able to prevent it, so give in and come visit him. It has to be."

Erec was now really angry and spurred his horse. "Let go of the bridle," he said, then threw back his cloak and drew his sword. He intended to cut off the hand of the mean coward, who well deserved this. Keii drew it back in time and fled without a fight. However, even though he was on Wintwalite, the best mount a knight ever had, he rode so slowly that he was overtaken. Fortunately for him, Erec noticed that he wore no armor and very quickly reversed his spear in order not to wound him: Keii profited greatly from his pursuer's good manners. Having turned the shaft toward Keii, Erec gave him such a blow that he fell from the horse like a sack, which would have been too bad for a noble knight, but was what he deserved.

[4734] When Erec led the horse away, the rascal Keii quickly ran after him crying loudly: "No, good knight! Show your noble spirit and let me keep it. Otherwise I shall be forever dishonored and scorned because, as God is my witness, it isn't mine." Erec turned around with a smile and listened to his lament. "Tell me, knight," he said, "what is your name and who owns this horse?" It can't hurt you to tell me who you are, and you needn't feel disgraced at having to do this, for it has happened to many men who were never fainthearted."

[4756] "Oh, no, sir!" replied Keii. "I implore you! If you want to show me kindness, then do so without stint by excusing me from giving my name. My cowardice here has brought me such shame that it would pain me very much to tell you, because I have indeed earned your disdain. For God's sake let it go."

"Nobody is here but you and me," said Erec, "so give your name, knight. There is no way out of it if you don't want to lose the horse." And he touched his own with the spurs as though he were about to ride off.

[4777] Keii begged him to wait and said, "I lament to God that I must proclaim my own dishonor. I'll tell you who I am: my name is Keii, and it pleases King Arthur to have me as lord high steward of his court. One of his nephews, the noble knight Gawein, lent me this horse. I am sorry he didn't refuse to do so, because I would have been spared the shame which I must now endure. I have only myself to thank that I couldn't just live peacefully: I looked for disgrace and found it in large measure. Today while the knight was eating, my unlucky star led me to ask for his horse, which he lent me at once. If he hadn't done it, I would not have suffered the dishonor that befell me. Well, no one can escape his fate. Noble knight, be kind and give me back the horse for God's sake or I'll be the laughingstock of everyone who sees me returning on foot."

[4807] "All right," said Erec. "I'll give it to you on one condition: you are to return it to Sir Gawein with my compliments. You must promise me this on your honor."

"I'll do it," replied Keii, and he did, for he was pleased that the affair had turned out so well. As he took back the horse, he said, "Since you have been so kind to me, worthy knight, I beg you to go further and let me know who you are: deign to tell me your name. It would be my gain and do you no harm. I would like to know because of your bravery. I would always regret having to part from you without learning your name or how to refer to you when I have pleasant memories of you. For God's sake tell me who you are."

[4831] "Not now," said Erec. "Perhaps you will find out later." The two then parted, each going his own way. Keii rode to the court, where his promise forced him not to keep silent but to relate truthfully the shameful story of what had happened. However, he described his misfortune so comically that his disgrace was taken as a joke and he was not ridiculed. When they were told of the knight's courage, all were very curious as to who it might be. "I couldn't learn who he was," spoke Keii, "for he wouldn't give his name. But I heard his voice—indeed he said a lot to me—and I would judge by it that he is Erec the son of King Lac." Everyone agreed that Keii was surely right.

[4860] "I would be very happy if he were brought to me," said King Arthur, "and would reward the one who brought him with my affection. Gawein, I assign the task to you and Keii. Up till now you both have so honored me that I can say only good of you. And if you do this, I shall value it more than all that you have done in the past to please me. Remember, Gawein, how things are between us, that you are my closest relative, and for my sake don't delay a moment longer, but help the queen and me to get to see Erec. Nothing more delightful could happen to me."

[4880] "My lord," answered Gawein, "you need not urge me, because I am quite willing to go. Truly there is no one whom I would rather see now than him. Should God in kindness let me overtake Erec, I assure you, sir, that I'll bring him back if I can possibly persuade him to come."

They rode off at once, and Keii led Gawein to the place where he had left the knight. The two hurried after him, following his trail at a gallop. As soon as they overtook Erec, the noble Gawein greeted him warmly in a cordial tone which contained no trace of anger and showed that his intentions were friendly. Gawein bade him good day and, when Erec thanked him, knew who he was and spoke his name at once. Overcome with joy at seeing the knight and pleasure at finding him strong and hearty, Gawein hugged him tightly. He welcomed him and his wife and expressed his sincere thanks for the friendly honor shown him in the matter of his horse, when Erec's loyalty had caused him to return it.

[4923] "My former comrade," Gawein then said to him, "we have chased after you through the forest, and if you would like to know why we were in such a hurry or what I want, I shall tell you. I beg you to show now whether you are fond of my lord and shall explain how. When our friend Keii brought my horse back to the court to me and, in relating his story, spoke of your valiant deed, we all wondered who could have done it, but with one voice guessed that it was you. Thereupon the queen and my lord at once urged us to hasten after you—that's why we galloped so—and bring you to their court. If you ever liked or esteemed King Arthur, do not reject his request, but be so kind as to visit him. That would make him the happiest man who ever lived. Don't hold back if you want to do him this favor: the rest of us would also be delighted."

[4959] Erec answered him thus: "Indeed, I owe the king so much that my heart will always be subject to him. If I fail to do as he desires and do not follow his wishes, it is not because I don't want to. However, I must refuse him this. Should the time come when it is necessary to risk everything for him, and it may well happen, I will show him my devotion. He will then have no doubt as to my feelings toward him. This time he should be kind enough to let me go, because I have renounced all pleasure for a while. Assure my lord and the queen of my willingness to serve them, keep them from being angry at me, and let me remain your faithful servant wherever I go."

[4984] Gawein was distressed when he saw that Erec would not yield. He motioned to his companion and whispered to him, saying, "Noble knight, show now such good will and skill that both my lord and I may be indebted to you. I have thought of the ruse which is most likely to succeed. I propose that you ride back at once and say that Erec won't come. Tell the king that if he wants to see him, it can be done only in this way: he should leave the place where he is and quickly move his camp to the far side of the forest where Erec must ride out. Meanwhile, I can surely delay him along the way so that he doesn't arrive there first."

[5013] "If you think it will work," said Keii, "I'll be glad to help," and he rode off forthwith and did just what Gawein had asked. When King Arthur heard the plan, he ordered that the meal be interrupted, hurried off as his nephew had advised, and pitched camp right beside the road, so that Erec could not pass without riding straight toward them. During this interval the worthy Gawein slowed Erec down by every stratagem he could think of until he had used up enough time with pleasantries for the king to get ahead of them. As often as his friend suggested that he go on back, he replied, "In a moment," until by fine deception he rode with him out of the forest just where the king was encamped by the way.

[5037] Erec was not pleased at the sight of all the tents, which covered a large field. He recognized them at once, for he had seen them often, and said, "What happened to me? I must have ridden in the wrong direction. This was your idea, Sir Gawein, and you haven't treated me well. I never heard of your playing such a mean trick before. I didn't intend to come here at all, and it was wrong of you to bring me. Who comes to court as little suited for courtly life as I am now would be better off at home. A man should be happy at court and behave accordingly. I cannot do that now and must abstain from courtly activity like one disabled. You can see that I am tired, wounded, and so unpresentable that I would gladly have stayed away if you had let me. You haven't dealt fairly with me."

[5068] Gawein responded kindly to his wrath. Embracing him, he said, "Don't be annoyed, sir. It is indeed better to lose a friend by good, sensible actions than to keep him by behaving otherwise. If he flares up in anger at first, he will see things right later and be fonder than ever of his comrade. What more can I say? Although I may have offended you, my intentions were good. You shall be my judge." Thus he cordially made his peace with Erec, and the latter's irritation and dismay subsided—the more quickly because he was shown more esteem and honor at the court than anyone had ever received before. It is plain that Arthur, the queen, and their entire retinue were glad to see him. Both Erec and Enite were welcome there. A stately reception was given the two who for a long time had suffered hardships on unknown roads.

[5100] When Enite came to Guinevere, the queen was most friendly. She took charge of her and led her away from her husband to her private tent, where they exchanged many questions and answers and lamented Enite's unusual troubles at length, as women do. For as long as she could the noble queen gave her comforts to make up for the privations she had endured. Meanwhile the knights conducted Erec to where, wounded and weary as he was, he could rest up. They removed his armor and gave him many highborn squires, none of whom would let himself be outdone by the others. All strove with equal zeal to serve him.

[5129] The queen soon came with all her ladies to visit him and express her sympathy. She brought a plaster which was very good for wounds, as I shall tell you. Men with mortal injuries had been saved by it. The wound on which it was bound ceased to pain and began to heal—not too quickly, but just right—and caused no further trouble. The plaster drove away everything evil while leaving the healthy flesh unharmed, and those who were cured by it had no scars: the skin was as smooth as if it had never been injured. There was never a better plaster anywhere than the one with which the queen bandaged the knight's side.

[5153] Is there anyone who is surprised and would like to hear where the plaster came from? Famurgan, the king's sister, had left it with him many years before, when she died. What great knowledge and marvelous arts were lost with her! She was a fairy, and it would be impossible to tell all the wonders she could do, or even half of them. However, I'll tell of her power as best I can. When she called on her magic, she could go around the whole world and return in an instant. I don't know who taught her that. Before I could turn a hand or wink an eye she would be gone and back again. She lived just as she pleased. She could hover in the air and rest there as easily as on the earth. She could dwell on the water and beneath it and was as much at home in the fire as in the dew: it made no difference to her. The lady could do all this. Moreover, whenever she wished, she could change a man into a bird or a beast and then quickly give him back his true form. She indeed knew a lot of magic.

[5190] Famurgan lived contrary to divine order, for the birds and wild beasts in forest and field obeyed her, and—what impresses me the most—even the evil spirits which are called demons were all under her control. She could perform wonders: the dragons of the air and the fish of the sea had to help with her projects. Besides, she had kindred deep in hell; the devil too was a friend who sent out of the fire as much aid as she wanted. She herself fearlessly seized plenty of whatever she desired from this earth. It bore no herb whose power she did not know as well as I know my own hand. Truly the world has known no greater master of magic arts than this Famurgan since the death of Sibyl and the demise of Erichtho, whose magic, according to Lucan, was such that her command could bring anyone she chose back to healthy life, even though he had long been dead—but I'll say no more about her now: it would be too much. As Famurgan was so wise, only a foolish man would be offended if she were to prepare a plaster for him. Indeed, I am sure that no matter how much one searched in medical books one would never find such powerful remedies as she used, against Christ's commandment, whenever she wished.

[5243] The fairy had applied all her skill in making the fine plaster with which the queen bound Erec's wound. He could easily feel its healing effect and, as soon as he was bandaged, began to think of resuming his journey. It seemed to him that he was well, and in spite of the many entreaties of the knights and ladies who came to visit him, he did not want to remain there longer. For the night, however, they gave their noble guest the best treatment they could, and would gladly have continued to do so if Erec had allowed it, which he did not. Since the requests of the king and queen did not help, there was no way for them to keep him longer than until early morning. No plea would serve.

[5270] When day dawned, all of them regretted that he would not postpone his departure for anyone. The king had breakfast early for his sake. Then the horses were brought up, and Erec took a courteous leave of the knights and ladies. One could tell by their behavior that everybody was fond of him and his wife, because both men and women wept with grief when the two departed. The king felt so bad that he didn't want to stay in the forest any longer and set out for Cardigan.

CHAPTER 4

Reconciliation

[5288] Erec now just followed the road, not knowing where it led: his only concern was to find adventure. He had ridden only a short time and had gone hardly a league when he heard from off the road the fearful screams of a woman in distress who was pitiably calling for help. As soon as he noticed the cries, Erec was eager to find out what the trouble was, which showed his bravery. He had Enite dismount at once and told her to wait for him there. Prompted by her heart, she commended him to God's care as he left her.

[5312] Guided only by the woman's voice, Erec made his way through the pathless, overgrown forest until he came to the place where she lamented in anguish in the rugged wilderness. With despairing hands the half-dead woman had ripped her headdress to pieces and had scratched and torn at herself until blood was running over her clothes and body. She was so beside herself with grief that anyone who had seen her then truly would have been moved to pity, no matter how unfeeling he might have been. The noble Erec almost wept at the sight of the poor, distraught woman. "Lady, for God's sake tell me why you are crying," he said, "and why you are all alone in this forest. Tell me quickly if I can help you." Bitter pain almost robbed her of her voice as uncontrollable sobbing interrupted her words so that she could hardly speak.

[5350] "I have good reason to weep, sir," she replied, "for my husband, the dearest man a woman ever had, is going to die."

"What happened, lady?" asked Erec.

"Sir, two giants took him from me and led him in this direction. They won't let him live, for they have hated him a long time. Oh, what cause I have to weep!"

"Have they gone far, lady?"

"Oh, no, dear sir."

"Then show me where they went."

"They rode that way, sir," and she pointed in the direction in which her husband had been taken.

[5368] "Cheer up, lady," said Erec. "I promise you that I shall either rescue him or die with him." With all her heart the good woman then commended him to God's protection. The prayer she said for the brave knight was long and earnest.

Erec found the trail and followed it as fast as he could until he caught sight of the two giants. They wore no armor and, unlike him, had neither shield nor spear nor sword, which, of course, was to his advantage. What were their weapons? Two long, heavy staffs with iron-studded heads. A timid man might very well avoid doing battle with them. The evil men also had two scourges with finger-thick cords with which they brutally drove their captive, who was completely naked.

[5402] His hands were tied behind his back, and his feet were bound together under the horse's belly. He received many blows as he rode before them. Indeed, they beat the poor man without mercy, so that from head to knee the skin hung down in shreds. The knight was horribly mistreated and with no respect for his station. If he had been a common thief, caught in the act, such a punishment would have been too severe. He had been whipped until he was faint from loss of blood and too weak to cry out. His blood ran down over the flanks of the horse, making it red all over. The man was in agony: no one could suffer greater torment than he did then and live.

[5429] When Erec saw this, he was so moved by the knight's distress that he changed color and would rather have died beside him than permit it to continue. "I don't wish to offend you lords," he said to the two giants, "but you must tell me for God's sake what the man whom you hold captive there has done to you. Tell me, what crime did he commit? I would like to know, and it will do you no harm to say. Is he a murderer or a thief? How did he earn from you such great punishment as he is suffering?" One of them replied, but scorned to answer the question: "Who are you to ask what he did to us, fool? We won't tell you. See how laughable you make yourself, you monkey, by asking so many questions that no one will answer. Why are you chasing after me?"

[5457] "I am not, sir," said Erec and, hoping to persuade them with guile to spare their captive, went on: "Believe me, sir, I did not follow you here as an enemy, but because I heard him crying out from afar and wanted to learn what was going on. You shouldn't be annoyed at that. However, to tell the truth—and I can't keep silent about this—if this is a nobleman, you should forever be ashamed of not treating him like one and not shunning this outrage. He has surely been punished enough for whatever he has done. For God's sake let him go."

[5476] "Your chatter bothers me," answered the giant, "and you had better stop asking questions if you value your life. If I could get any honor or fame out of you, I would wring your neck like a chicken's. What good are your questions doing him? Treat him as a kinsman and help him: he needs it." With this he struck his captive before Erec's eyes and told the latter to be on his way. Once more Erec tried to persuade him to let the knight go, but his request was useless and only made the giants angry. To spite him they beat the man worse than before, since they weren't afraid of Erec and didn't think he dared fight them.

[5498] The bold warrior was incensed to see the knight suffering because of him. Without waiting longer, he bravely took his spear under his arm, spurred his horse, and charged at them in a rage. They weren't at all worried, and one was so careless in his disdain that he got a spear in his head. It was thrust with such force that all but a yard of the shaft went through his eye. For all his scorn, he was struck down dead, as God in his courtliness decreed.

[5518] When his companion saw the huge fellow crash down, he turned his staff around, seized it with both hands, and came angrily toward Erec. The knight dismounted, which pleased the giant, who assumed that he had already won. God let his hope deceive him. He flailed away like a madman, and Erec would have been killed at once if he had not been on his guard and had not known how to protect himself skillfully. He was nimble enough to stay out of reach and catch the blows with his shield, which suffered greatly. Wherever it was struck, the hard wood became so soft that it broke in three pieces and the studs flew in all directions.

[5541] However, the staff was so heavy that the giant bent far over with every blow and could not pull it back at once. Before he was ready to strike again, Erec's quickness had taken him in close and away again: in this manner he wounded his enemy four times in the leg. This did not bother him until a fifth blow cut it off entirely. When the huge rogue sank to his knee, Erec sprang at him, but the devil still fought boldly. He swung at Erec so often and so fiercely that we may well wonder how the knight survived. To be sure, he who gave David the strength to defeat Goliath was with him and helped him gain the victory. The struggle ended as Erec beat the giant to the ground and cut off his head.

[5570] By the time Erec had triumphed, the captive's horse had carried him into the forest, and no one could have known where to find him. It was the grass and the trees that put the knight on the trail and showed where the other had ridden. Since he was bound, he could not avoid the trees or keep from brushing against them, and everything he touched as the horse bore him along was red with his blood. Erec followed this trail of blood a long ways until he overtook the poor man. Then he untied his feet and hands and brought him back to his wife as he had found him: bloody from the scourges, but otherwise unharmed. He had no reason to complain, for he recovered from his painful ordeal and came through alive.

[5600] At the sight of him, the lady's heart was filled with both joy and grief, which do not go well together. She was distressed to see her husband covered with blood, for she was not used to worrying about him and had never seen him in such a state. That he should return alive, however, brought happiness that conquered her sorrow. The lady's mood changed like glass which is cleaned after being covered with black paint: when the paint comes off, what before was dark becomes clear and beautiful. Her heart thus became a bright mirror, freed of its former care and lifted up to the light with pure joy, as if it had never known sorrow.

[5628] The loving couple was very happy and thanked Erec

repeatedly. "Sir," they said, "since we owe our lives to you, we want to be your vassals."

"I would be forever pleased to have served you, sir," Erec answered the knight, "and, if I have not done so already, I shall in the future, God willing, for that is my desire. I ask no other reward than that you do me the honor of telling me your name." The knight said that he was Cadoc of the land of Tafriol and told how the two monsters happened to capture him. He had wanted to travel from his country to Britain in order to present his wife and himself to the king's retinue. The giants, who had long been his bitter enemies—I don't know why—learned that he would be going through the forest, lay in wait for him along the road, and seized him as he rode up.

[5662] On hearing the knight's account, Erec tried to restore his pride with kindly guile. "Sir," he said, "you shouldn't fret about what these giants did to you. No one who wants to do brave deeds can forever escape having something happen to him of which he is ashamed, but he gets over it. How often I've been treated worse!" He consoled him with these words and then said, "I would advise you not to let anyone keep you from traveling to Britain as you had planned. I tell you truly how it is there: in no other land can a knight gain as much fame. Who does well there is a lucky man. Now I ask that you do me this one honor. When you get to the court, take your wife by the hand and go before the queen to pay my respects. Tell her what it is that you want and say that I sent you to join her retinue. My name is Erec—she knows me well." Cadoc promised that he would, and they parted.

[5700] The knight then went to the court and did as Erec wanted. He presented himself to the queen just as he had been asked to do and took up her service. The queen wished Erec the best of fortune as a reward.

The noble Erec quickly left the forest and looked for the place where he had told Enite to wait for him. He had fought so hard that his wounds had broken open, and the loss of blood together with the weakening effect of the blows made him deathly pale and robbed him of his strength until he barely managed to ride back to where the lady waited. If it had been any farther, he would not have made it, as soon became apparent.

[5730] The knight was so faint that when he leaned forward to dismount—for he wanted to get some rest—he came down head first and fell with such force that he lay there as if dead. His fall filled Enite with bitter pain and deep distress. In her misery she raised a pitiful, despairing cry which was loud enough to resound from the forest. However, only the echo that the trees sent back undiminished to the field joined in her lament. It alone helped her bewail her grief, since no one else was there. The noble lady threw herself upon Erec and kissed him. She then struck her breasts, kissed him again, and cried out: every second word was "Oh!" She tore her hair and beat herself, as women do to express their anguish. When faced with calamity, they do not fight against it, but use eyes and hands to weep and punish themselves; they can't do otherwise. I therefore pray that misfortune may strike whoever causes them pain, for this is neither right nor manly.

[5774] Enite raged at God, saying, "Lord, if it is your will that such a good knight should lose his life because of his noble nature, then a strange anger has robbed you of pity. I have heard that you are full of compassion, yet you show little of it to poor me. If you can be sorry for me, now is the time. Look at my husband lying there badly wounded, perhaps dead. Have mercy on me, for my heart has died and I am in great need: see how sadly I stand here. Pity me, Lord, because it is pitiable that I, thus deserted, should live longer in such misery. Were it not that all your works are blameless, Lord, I would charge you with a mistake here, because you permit me to go on living after you have taken from me the only one for whom I should live.

[5803] "Lord, if you are able to prove that you can see into all hearts and that nothing can be concealed from you, in mercy do it. If I have forfeited this knight in any way since he became my husband, by thought or deed, so that it is fitting that your power should take him from me, then I agree that justice has prevailed and that I deserve to lose him. However, if I have done nothing of the kind, you ought to reward me in kindness, Lord, by having mercy on me and letting him live. Should you not want to give him back to me, then remember, Lord, the well-known teaching you have proclaimed which I beg you to support, that a man and his wife should be one body. Do not separate us, for this would be a grave injustice to me: show your great compassion and help me to die here.

[5833] "Come, one of you hungry beasts of prey—wolf, bear, or lion—and devour us both so that our one body may not go different ways. And may God care for our souls, which indeed will not part whatever happens to the body." Since none came, she cried out to them again: "Foolish beasts, you have killed many sheep and swine, the livestock of poor peasants who didn't want you to have them and couldn't stand the loss. If you were clever, you would get all you wanted to eat here, for I'll willingly deliver myself to you, which should please you. Come now, I'll be glad to have you seize me. Where are you? Here I am."

[5857] Her calls were in vain, because no wild beasts heard them and came. But I am sure that if one had come and observed her sad manner, were it ever so hungry, it would have shown how much she was to be pitied by helping her to bewail her sorrow. Against her will she survived. When she realized that she was not to have such a death, she lamented more despairingly than before and was at the point of killing herself. No greater misery was ever seen.

[5875] "My dear husband," she said, "since I must lose you, I hereby forever renounce all men except the one in my heart whom I suddenly find so attractive and love with all my being. If I could win his affection, I would make him a loyal wife. I mean you, dearest Death. It is for love of you that I go against custom and do the courting, even though I am a woman. Take me, dear Death, for I need your love. Oh how happy I, poor woman, would be in your arms! I am the bride for you. Why don't you take me quickly? Since you must get me sometime, I advise you to do it now. I am just the right wife for you—still young and beautiful, at the best time of life—and you cannot come for me too soon. What use would you have for me later, when grief and old age have robbed me of beauty and youth? What would you want with me then? But now I am still fit for a nobleman."

[5908] After she had spoken at length and had not been able to get her way and persuade Death with her plea to take her into his realm, she scolded him, as women do, saying whatever she wished. "May evil befall you, wicked Death!" she said, "A curse on you! How often you display your wantonness. It is true what everyone says: that you are treacherous. You strive to harm him who has never deserved suffering. I have seen much of that from you. You have bad advisers, for you suddenly take the life of a man whom the world cannot do without and spare another whose end is desired by all, letting him reach old age. You use your power foolishly. You have felled a noble knight here and not disposed of me in such a way as to warrant my ever speaking well of you. I don't know where to turn now in my misery. I was born of misfortune and have lost both body and soul—just as a woman deserves for such a great misdeed, who has betrayed her husband as I have mine. But for me he would not have died.

[5949] "He never would have thought of this sad journey if I had suppressed the mournful sigh I uttered that day when I lay beside him and believed him asleep. Cursed be the day on which I started all this! I have destroyed my happiness, honor, and well-being. Oh what misfortune has befallen me! Well, fool that I am, what do I gain by talking about it? God gave me just the life I wanted, with all my heart desired, and I acted like the fools who stupidly begrudge themselves their own fame and wealth. They cannot endure it when things go well with them but must take the advice of the devil—who is glad to get rid of their honor—and destroy their own happiness.

[5974] "Oh, dear mother and father! You don't yet know my great sorrow. You both believed that you had much improved my state, which was to be expected, since you gave me in marriage to a mighty king. The good fortune for which you hoped has been lost. Whoever thinks that God's purpose can be turned aside is mistaken, because no cunning can help: one must let his will prevail. I, too, must do so, and I am destined to be unhappy. I can tell this indeed by the bitter hardships I have suffered up till now. He has condemned the body of this poor woman, that is easy to see, but I cannot know what he intends for my soul. Whatever happens to my body, I will not lament if my soul is saved. I now understand something which I have often heard, that an unlucky man's fortune will not improve no matter how one tries to help him.

[6008] "Who takes a linden tree from the roadside where it is not cared for, plants it in his garden, and by tending it well tries to make up for its earlier neglect in dry soil—with the belief that he can raise a good fruit tree from it in his orchard—could not be more fully deceived by a dream. No matter how zealous he may be, it can never be made to bear better fruit than is its nature to produce, than it bore before it was dug up from the poor soil by the road where no one bothered with it. No matter how beautiful and splendid the tree is, one can waste a lot of manure and hoeing on it. One should use me as an example of this, Godforsaken as I am. God has so cursed me that if my great misfortune moved everyone to pity and I were crowned queen of all women, I would still suffer from grief as long as I lived unless he brought it to an end.

[6042] "Since God has taken from me the dearest husband a woman ever had, Death must accept the outcome even though he does not want me. I shall be faithful to him and shall find a way to join his retinue whether he likes it or not. Why should I hurry to fall at his feet just because he doesn't want me? I can easily give myself right here that for which I begged him, and I won't wait any longer but do it. Truly, I have made the right decision."

[6062] She reached down to the ground, seized her husband's sword, and drew it from its sheath. Her grief was such that she wanted to kill herself with it and thus foolishly avenge his death on herself, but God forbade this and saved Enite's life with kind wisdom by causing her to curse the sword as soon as she saw it. It was a wonder that her heart did not break with sorrow. In the fury of despair her voice broke—ringing now high, now low—and the forest resounded fearfully with her cries, with an often repeated "Oh! Oh!"

[6084] Looking at the sword, she wailed loudly, "Oh, cursed be the hour when you were made! You killed my husband: you are to blame for his death. He would never have sought out frightful dangers, here or elsewhere, were it not for his trust in you. That's how you took him from me. My dear lord risked his life in many a conflict which he would have avoided if he had not relied so much on you. He often praised you, and now you have failed him. I don't know whether you regret having broken faith with him, but you will pay for it. You won't get off easily, because you will have to commit another murder."

[6110] It became clear that she meant this when she placed the tip of the sword against her breast and, wishing to die, prepared to fall on it. Just then a man—sent by God—rode up and stopped her. It was a mighty count whose castle was nearby, Oringles of Limors, whom God had chosen to save her. Luckily for her, he had gone out and was riding through the forest. I don't know why, but my heart tells me that it was to rescue her that he rode forth with many knights that day. By chance he entered the forest by the road where Erec was lying in such a sorrowful state with Enite watching over him. While still a long way off, the nobleman heard the woman tormenting herself with cries of distress and, curious to see what was happening, came up just as she placed the sword against her breast to kill herself.

[6149] When he rode near, the count saw by her appearance that Enite was going to stab herself and sprang hastily from his horse. He almost came too late, after the blade had done its work. He quickly seized her, averted the deed, and tore the sword from her hands. Throwing it away, he said, "Tell me, strange woman, why did you want to take your life and thereby destroy the loveliest creature of any kind that a man's eyes ever saw?" Enite could hardly reply. "Dear sir," she said, "you can see yourself what is wrong."

"Were you going to kill yourself?"

"Sir, I had no choice."

"Was he your husband or your lover?"

"Both, sir."

"Well tell me who killed him."

[6175] While Enite told the full story of what had happened, the count was thinking that he had never in his life seen a more beautiful woman, near or far. His knights confirmed his opinion when he left her and went to have a short talk with them. "You can readily observe one thing about this lady," he said to his companions; "wherever the knight may have found her or however she may have come here, she is truly of noble birth. Her beauty is proof of that. Now give me your advice. You know my situation, that I have no wife. I am strongly inclined to marry this lady: I think she would be a good mistress for my country and I was sure at once that she is from a noble family. Moreover,

my heart has chosen her. I now ask for your assent and hope that
you will not object but all be as pleased as I. If this should be the
case, I shall gladly be indebted to you the rest of my life." They
all consented, and the count was happy to take their advice.

[6213] He then did his best to console Enite, as one comforts a
friend who has suffered grief. "Lovely lady," he said, "why do
you torture yourself so fiercely? For God's sake and mine, too,
control yourself a little more than you have. I admit that you are
only acting as women do, and I think it right for you to mourn
your husband, for you show your faithfulness by this. However,
you have lamented enough, because it can't do you any good. I
think the best way to treat a great loss is to find solace early, for
a lengthy sorrow only gives one a troubled spirit. Think about it,
beautiful woman. If you could restore him to life by weeping, we
would all help you lament and share your pain, but, sad to say,
this can't be. Moreover, if appearances do not deceive me, your
husband was not so highborn or rich, so strong, handsome, or
esteemed that you would be unable to make up for your misfortune. Indeed, you will be fully compensated for him if you do as I
say.

[6251] "It appears that God sent me to you at a lucky time with
all the aid you need. Often what a person assumes to be a great
harm changes easily to something desirable, and this is true of
the loss you think you have suffered here today, because you will
gain much honor through it. Your poverty indeed will turn to
wealth. I am a count and lord of a mighty land of which you shall
be mistress. See, your husband's death is a blessing and leads to
your good fortune, because now everything will go very well
with you. I am not married and want to have you as my wife.
This life will suit you better than traveling about the country
with only a single man to protect you, which is not what you
deserve. I shall make knights, ladies, and squires subject to
you—more powerful vassals than any other count ever had—if
you will just stop weeping."

[6282] Grief-stricken and angry, Enite could answer only as
her heart dictated. "Sir," she replied, "say no more. Be happy
that you are rich and for God's sake do not laugh at my poverty.
Hear my resolve, which I shall state briefly. I shall never be your
wife or anyone else's, now or later, if I can help it, unless God

gives me back my husband. The first I had will also be the last. Believe me, sir, for it will end that way."

[6302] "That is how women talk," the count said to the knights, "so one shouldn't reprove her. She will get over her despondence, and I'll see that it turns out well." He was very pleased with the lady. He then told the knights there to cut poles for a horse-borne stretcher. It was soon ready, and Erec was placed on it like a dead man. He was taken to Limors, where the count gave him as large a watch as he could and ordered candles brought which were to burn at his head until the burial. It is no wonder that Enite was sorely distressed, because she thought he was dead.

[6324] The count was strongly affected by the sight of her in all her beauty and could not wait until her husband was buried, but wanted to make her mistress of his country that very night. Although his entire retinue thought it unseemly, he sent messengers throughout the land to summon those lords whose duty it is to act in God's name to come and give the lady to him, for the count didn't believe he could endure further delay. Love's might is so great that he wanted to lie with her that very night. All the clergy came who could be found that day, including bishops and abbots, and the lady was given to the count, even though this was against her will and she found it grievous and loathsome. He insisted on marrying her, and her protests were in vain. He had high hopes, but God had the power.

[6352] It was now time for the evening meal, and the lord of the castle was glad it was so late, for he was looking forward to the night, which he expected to spend most pleasantly with the lady. Still, it may not turn out that way: I myself would not care if his hopes deceived him. The count went to the table and, after sitting down, sent two chaplains and three vassals to where the lady was keeping watch over her husband, who was lying on a bier, to ask her to come to the feast. I doubt that it did any good, because she didn't even look their way when one of them spoke to her. They told this to the count, who sent many more lords to her. He did so to honor the lady, believing that she would be the more likely to respond to the notice that the meal was ready, but she was so heartsick that she didn't see the messengers at all.

[6377] "I must go myself," said the count. He then went to her, took her hand, and said that she should come to the table with him. The lady asked him to excuse her, saying, "It would be most unwomanly if I were to feast now and forget so quickly the dearest husband a wife ever had. Oh, how unseemly that would be!"

"What are you saying?" he replied. "There is no need for you to mourn like this. You have lost a husband whom, God willing, I shall fully replace, and I shall gladly devote my life and wealth to you to make up for your sorrow. That is my intention, but you prevent me with behavior which does not become you and has made it impossible all day for anyone to comfort you. The opposition which you stubbornly maintain is foolish. Your loss is not so great: my station is surely as high as his and probably higher. Come, my lady, and I shall place in your hands my lands, myself, and such great wealth that you can forget your poverty and sorrow. Just come with me to the table."

[6412] "God forbid that I should thus forsake my companion," she replied and took a solemn oath: "Since God has deprived me of my husband, I shall never take another. I would rather be committed to the earth with him than do so."

"Stop such talk," he said, "as a favor to me, and come to eat. I insist on it." However, no matter how much he urged her, she would not leave until he used force. He pulled her away against her will: she was not strong enough to prevent it. Instead of seating the lady at his side, he ordered that a folding chair be set up for her opposite him so that he could better look at her. Although the count often pressed her to eat, Enite could not forget her dear husband. She grieved constantly, wringing her hands in misery and weeping until the table before her was wet with tears. The lord entreated her again and again to control herself, but she could not stop.

[6446] "Lady," he then said, "you are persisting in making both of us miserable and also my esteemed guests, who came here to enjoy themselves. If you weren't being childish, you would stop lamenting, and if you could only understand how much your state has improved in just a short time, you wouldn't be at all troubled. I never knew anything so strange as the fact that you can neither be quiet nor admit that your situation has greatly improved and is indeed very good. Anyone who has been as lucky as you have here would do better to sing than weep and complain. I must tell you frankly that you are grieving too long and that you are much better off today than you were yesterday.

[6471] "You were poor before and now are rich, were little esteemed and now God has granted you honor, were unknown and now rule over a country. Formerly you made a poor appearance and were not respected, now you are a grand lady, a mighty countess. You wandered aimlessly and without comforts until your good fortune led you to me and a life of splendor. You endured many hardships and lived wretchedly, but God has led you away from that and given you all you could desire. There was much to trouble you before, and no one cared about you; now you should praise God for rescuing you and stop your foolish bewailing, because you have more than any other woman of your land. If you want to know, you are punishing yourself needlessly. You lost a poor man and got me in his place: you should be happy with such an exchange. I would give all women the advice, which couldn't displease them, that they accept a rich husband for such a one as you had. Now I order you to stop this folly and eat."

[6507] "Sir," replied the noble queen, "you have told me much that might as well have been left unsaid, because all your talking will do no good. I'll give you a short answer which you can believe: I swear that no food will enter my mouth until my dead husband eats." The count could no longer restrain himself and now showed his base nature as his anger led him to great folly and crude behavior. He struck Enite with his hand so hard that the blood gushed forth and cried, "Eat, you slut!"

[6525] Everyone thought this very ill-mannered and said so. Many reproved the count to his face, others found fault with him among themselves, maintaining that it was a stupid act which he might better have left undone. He was strongly condemned. They rebuked him until the wicked man was enraged, for he could not endure being blamed. "It is strange that you lords should find fault with the way I treat my wife," he said fiercely, "for no one has a right to say anything, good or bad, about a man's actions toward his wife. She belongs to me and I to her. How will you keep me from dealing with her as I please?" With this he silenced them all.

[6550] Let us tell you how the lady acted when she was struck: for the first time that day she was pleased. Since blows seldom make one happy, perhaps you would like to hear what made her feel that way. She was happy because she would a thousand times rather die than live, and the blow, with a man's strength behind it, gave her hope that she would be freed of her life, that the count would avenge whatever else she said with blows until he killed her. She therefore began to lament without restraint and wail loudly, thinking that this would cause her death. She moved away from him and cried, "Believe me, sir, I care nothing for your blows. I'll never be your wife, no matter what you do to me, not even if you kill me. You can be sure of that."

[6577] She went on thus until he struck her roughly on the mouth again. She did not attempt to avoid the blow, but moved toward him in order to get more of them. She hoped to have her wish fulfilled. "Oh what an unfortunate woman I am!" she exclaimed. "If my companion were alive, I wouldn't have to endure this beating."

At the time Enite began to wail so loudly, Erec was lying senseless and as if dead, although he was not. He had recovered somewhat, but was still in a faint when her outcry caused him to start up in alarm, like one who awakes frightened from a bad dream. He sat up on the bier and looked about bewildered, wondering what had happened to him and how he had gotten there. Then he heard her again as she called loudly, "Oh my dear lord! You are dead, and I cry for your help in vain." He knew who she was as soon as Enite called to him and could tell that she was in some sort of danger, but did not know what or where it was. He did not stay on the bier any longer after recognizing her voice, but sprang to his feet in a rage and stormed swiftly into the group. There were many swords nearby, hanging on a wall. Seizing one, Erec killed the count and the two men sitting beside him in the first rush. The others fled. No attention was paid to good manners—no one stepped back and said, "After you, sir"—but whoever could get free dashed away.

[6630] This is how it was. The laymen didn't wait for the clergy—no matter how high the rank that went with the tonsure, be he abbot or bishop, he had no precedence—and servants crowded ahead of their masters. The entire court fled. Pushing throngs were dammed up before the doors, and the passage through them seemed very long—a step was like a league. I myself have never attended such a wedding. The hurried retreat became a rout, in which many noble warriors hid under benches in a most unknightly manner. There is one thing that happens often and does not surprise me: who fears for his life usually flees from the valley up to the castle to save himself from turmoil. These, however, were flying out of the castle and crawling into holes like mice.

[6656] The wide gates, the outer as well as the inner, were too narrow for the swarm, so that, driven by terrible fear, people came falling down over the walls like hail. Limors was left deserted. They had good reason to flee since they feared death, but their flight was not a disgrace. Whoever defamed them because of it would be too hasty. Now tell me. If a dead man with bloody wounds, laid out for burial with head and hands covered by grave cloths and feet wrapped in bands, should suddenly charge at a group, sword in hand and shouting a battle cry, wouldn't anyone run who valued his life? As brave as I am, I would have fled had I been there. No one dared to stand and wait for him except Enite, who was very happy to see the dead man. All her troubles changed to pleasure, and she was filled with joy.

Erec took her by the hand and searched hurriedly until he found his armor, a shield, and a spear. Then he armed himself just as if he had never been injured; however, he didn't find their horses. "Oh what bad luck!" he cried. "Must we go on foot? We have never done that before." Let us now pray God to send these strangers in a foreign land, Erec and Enite, a horse to carry them.

[6702] When he found nothing to ride, he did the best he could. He hung his shield from his neck, took the spear in his left hand, and, with Enite at his right side, hurried out of the gate. Just then his horse was brought to him, which he no more expected than did the one who rode it. This clearly showed how lucky he was. The count's page had taken it to the water and gaily sang a rotruange as he was riding it back up the castle road, for he knew nothing of what had happened.

[6723] Erec recognized the horse as soon as he saw it and was very pleased: this was God's doing. He waited quietly until the horse came close enough. Then he seized it by the bridle, took possession of it, and started out. Since they had only the one horse, he placed Enite in front of him and thought he would ride straight through the country. However, the night was dark, he did not know the way, and he was afraid that they might suffer shame and injury from the inhabitants when they learned what he had done. So, with the help of Enite, who guided him, he went back along the road which he had traversed on the stretcher. This was for safety's sake.

[6750] Three lands lay near each other—that in which Erec had killed the count, that of the little man who had wounded him, and that of King Arthur—and were separated only by the forest in which Erec was riding after this last trouble. After they had entered the forest and, free of their worries, were again on a familiar road, King Erec asked Enite how he had gotten into the power of the count of whose slaying I have told you. Red-eyed and weeping, she related the story to him. A sudden end then came to the painful test to which he had needlessly subjected her in that he had not spoken kindly to her since they had left home.

[6778] The result of Enite's trial was quite clear, and Erec had no doubt about it. He had wanted to find out if she was a good wife and had fully tried her as one refines gold in a crucible, so that he was now sure that she was faithful and trustworthy, a woman without fault. He pressed the noble Enite to his breast, gave her many loving kisses, and begged her to forgive him for the friendless life and many hardships she had endured on the journey. Erec promised that everything would improve, and indeed kept his vow. Since he asked her so fondly, she pardoned him at once, saying, "Dear lord, none of the many troubles were hard to bear but one: truly the others were nothing compared with the distress of being separated from you. I would soon have died if I had had to suffer that any longer."

[6814] But look here. When the wondrous event took place at Limors Castle, a page escaped and ran away through the forest to bring the news at once to the little king who was so brave. This was the Guivreiz of whom I have told you before, the one who wounded Erec. The boy knew the way very well and went as fast as he could. Moreover, he did not have far to go, since there was only the forest between the two lands.

[6830] When he pounded on the castle gate, he did not have to wait, but was admitted at once. He then went before the king, who had not yet gone to bed, and told him how Count Oringles had been slain by a dead man. Guivreiz finally guessed by the way the story went that this was Erec. "Oh! Oh!" he cried loudly. "What a misfortune it would be if the best knight alive were to be killed. May God protect him, because the count's countrymen will murder him right away as soon as they learn the truth. If I could stand in front of my friend, I would surely do it. God willing, I shall try." He armed himself without delay and also the knights who were with him, thirty in all. Their horses were brought, and, filled with anxiety and grief, the king hurried toward the forest to help the knight escape from the foreign land.

[6862] It happened that both chose the same road: Erec at one end, the king at the other. Since they were riding in opposite directions, they could not help but meet—as indeed fate would have it—and since neither knew he was approaching the other, Erec was in great danger. He became aware of the armed band while it was still far off because of the loud clatter of the shields. "Lady, I hear a large troop riding toward us," he said to Enite, "and I don't intend to turn aside without a fight, like a coward. I haven't much strength but will fight them as well as I can. Get down on the road until you see what happens." I believe the lady was more distressed now than ever before, for she saw how weak he was.

[6892] Erec stayed in the road while the others approached, and the moon came out from behind the clouds to brighten the night. The king, who was at the head of the band, saw him blocking the way. Erec quickly prepared for battle: may God protect him! What do you think the king did? He too got ready because he had to joust or show a lack of courage, and I can tell you truly that he was no coward. He proved it there and often elsewhere. They lowered their spears and showed their skill, charging at each other in a splendid joust. Both of the worthy knights struck their targets squarely, and only the strength of the one who was more rested gave him success and the victory. He struck Erec to the ground a full spear-length behind his horse and then dismounted beside him. Enite was in despair.

[6926] This had never happened to Erec till then—none could claim without lying that he had been unhorsed before—and it would also not have occurred to the good knight this time if he had been well. But, as things stood, his strength was gone and he had to suffer defeat at the hands of the king, who was now untying Erec's helmet with the intention of killing him. Enite could not let that happen. Without a moment's delay she sprang from the concealment of the hedgerow where she had been standing anxiously and threw herself over her companion.

"No, good sir!" she cried. "If you ever had a knightly spirit, don't kill my husband! I tell you that he is badly injured, and it would be a disgrace, a sin, for you to do anything more to him. A King Guivreiz—I believe that is his name—wounded him in the side."

[6957] Guivreiz recognized Enite by her voice and also because she had mentioned his name. He stepped back quickly and said, "Lady, tell me who this knight is and where you met me, for I am the one of whom you spoke. I am afraid I have done something wrong. Lady, tell me who you are. Are you Lady Enite, and is this knight Erec? I can't wait long since I came out because of him. I received news of him that worried me: that he was in trouble nearby, at Limors. What I heard made me fear that he would be killed if I and my companions did not set out at once to help him. But I am lingering too long here in the forest. I must get to him right away. It would be a pity if he were slain."

Enite told the king who they were, showed him proof, and thus saved her husband's life. He recognized Erec as soon as she took off his cap. Guivreiz was delighted to see him and said, "Welcome, my lord. Tell me, are you all right or are you hurt?"

[6995] "There is nothing the matter with me," replied Erec. "I am unharmed except for the wound you gave me before." The king was pleased to hear this and took off his own helmet. Then the two men ran joyfully to one another and kissed each other in true friendship. Guivreiz was full of remorse because of the trouble he had caused Erec in the joust, but when he spoke of it, Erec answered, "Say no more and don't be concerned about it. You didn't treat me wrongly. If a man behaves foolishly, it is fitting that he receive a fool's reward. Since I was so imprudent and arrogant as to want to take control of someone else's road and hold it alone against many brave knights, you gave me what I deserved. My penalty was too light when one considers that I, just by myself, wanted to gain honor at the expense of all of you. I should have been punished much more."

[7024] They let the matter drop, and Guivreiz bowed to Enite and welcomed her. She thanked him. Now that it was clear that Erec's life was not in danger, all of them were happy. They mounted but did not ride far. With thoughtful concern the king led them away from the road to a meadow, where they spent the night so that Erec could rest and regain some of his strength. Because of their situation, they had a good fire. This wasn't hard since there was plenty of wood. One only needed to gather it.

[7046] Relieved from care, they sat by the fire, and Erec recounted the troubles he had had since riding away from Guivreiz after they had wounded each other—I have already told you all I know about this. The knights lamented the hardships of their dear guests and fervently thanked God that Erec was still alive, for his life had hovered in the balance like a shipwrecked man in the waves of the sea swimming on a plank to shore. He had often been in straits as desperate as this. However, God and his own bravery had brought him from the stormy waters of peril to the strand of good fortune, so that his sorrows had been overcome and he was very happy. He was still lucky: may God continue to help him.

[7079] It was now time to go to sleep, and all the knights looked around to find the best place to prepare a bed for Erec. On one side of the fire they saw three large, well-formed beeches of equal height, with thick foliage and wide-spreading branches. Under one of them they made a couch apart from the rest for Erec and Enite, who for a long time had not lain beside each other and had neither slept nor eaten together. The foolish discord came to an end, and they began a better life. A bed was prepared for the king under the next beech, which stood in the middle, and the knights camped under the third.

[7106] "Tell me, what did they use for bedding?"

Truly, just what the forest offers: beautiful leaves and fresh grass, the best that could be found there. But, as long as they did sleep, why ask a lot of questions?

The night came to a pleasant end, and they rode forth with the

dawn. In order to care for them better, their host, the small
Guivreiz, led Erec and Enite to one of his strongholds nearby,
where he knew they would be safe and very comfortable. There
was an abundance of all good things here, as I shall explain.

[7124] The castle stood in the middle of a lake which supplied
more than enough of the best fish of all kinds ever brought to a
king's table. Moreover, the best hunting we have ever heard
about was here. The king had enclosed over two leagues of the
forest around the lake with a wall, so that it opened only on the
water. This circle, as I can tell you, was divided by other walls
into three equal parts. One held many red deer, in another there
were wild boars. Would you like to know about the third part?
There was only small game in it: foxes, hares, and the like. The
preserve was fully stocked, and no one who wanted to hunt could
ever complain that he found no game.

[7155] The lord of this hunting castle also kept many well-
trained hounds here. Whenever he looked out and saw men
hunting with them, he could watch the chase as well while
sitting on the battlements as those could who were taking part.
Who could blame him if he sometimes wanted to watch the
hounds running while looking down from the castle with the
ladies, for the last run of whatever red deer was started was
always to the water of the lake, and it was never caught anywhere else but there below the castle. Who wanted to hunt boar
or bear found many strong, broad spears for his use, and if he
wanted to hunt hares, he could find the best of harriers, as I have
told you. Now as for you: hunt anything you wish. There are
hounds and game here and all that one needs for hunting: nets,
good bows and throwing spears, and whatever else your heart
desires. One could entertain himself well here.

[7188] The name of this castle was Penefrec, and it lacked
nothing. There was plenty of fish, roast game, wheat bread,
wine, and everything else, also a lot of fine bedding. That is why
the king brought his noble guest here to rest: he wanted to be
sure that Erec and Enite regained their health and strength. As
a reward for his bravery, Erec was treated as a highly honored
guest, and both he and Enite received good care.

[7207] Who will be the doctor to heal his wounds? This could be done by two highborn ladies, the king's noble and beautiful sisters, who were very happy that Erec had ridden to them in such straits that he would have to accept their service. They were just the doctors for him: they healed his wounds because they knew how to do it. The kind Lady Enite also watched over him with faithful concern. With the help of all three, Erec's side was completely cured. The sisters had some of the plaster of which I have already told you, that Famurgan made. Lady Guinevere had sent it to them as a gift, which was lucky for the knight.

[7232] King Erec remained at Penefrec Castle until he had recovered from his wound and was completely healed, exactly fourteen days. When he had all of his strength back, he wanted to start out again, since he did not feel at ease there even though it was very comfortable and pleasant. The noble knight was as eager to leave soon as if he were alone in a forest without shelter or any comforts and exposed to wind and rain. That was because nothing in the world gave him more pleasure than knightly deeds, performed with vigor by his own hands. This was the life he had chosen, and he liked it: it was his food and sleep. The fourteen days indeed seemed to him like many years. He did not want to stay longer and would have ridden away before if he had been able.

[7264] Poor Enite! What is the good, beautiful, highborn lady to ride now? As you heard earlier, she lost her palfrey when Count Oringles was killed at Limors and she and Erec barely escaped from there. However, the loss was made good, for it was replaced and in such a manner that she will never need to complain—with one which I shall describe, since it was as pretty as anybody has ever had or shall ever see. The king's two sisters gave it to Enite and were very pleased that she was willing to accept it from them. In fact, it just suited her.

[7284] Does someone want to know whether the palfrey was better than that she rode before? They are not to be compared. This is what the new one looked like with its contrasting markings. The left side was gleaming white—it could not have been whiter—and so splendid that the luster dazzled the eyes. No one could look at it steadily for long, so I have heard. The other side

was as different as could be. There was no white here: it was as
black as the left side was white. The palfrey was therefore black
and white.

[7309] These opposing colors were nicely separated by a line
running between them which was about half a finger's breadth
and as green as grass. Beginning at the nose, it went back like a
brush stroke between the ears, straight through the mane,
along the backbone to the tail, and likewise down the chest and
back between the forelegs in the same manner: it was quite
unusual. There was a ring of the same color around each eye.
The mane was soft, curly, and just the right thickness and
length: it hung down almost to the knees. The long forelock was
divided by the green stripe into black and white halves, as was
also the tail.

[7336] Since I have already told you something of the palfrey's
appearance, I'll go on and tell you the rest. It was just the right
size: neither too high nor too low, too long nor too short, too
stocky nor too slender. The narrow head was carried high, as is
proper, and had short, protruding ears—one white, the other
black, with the white ear enclosed by a black ring and the black
one by a white ring. The powerful neck lifted up in a nice curve,
becoming thinner where it joined the head: it was in every
respect a joy to see. The chest was broad and muscular, the legs
were smooth and straight—neither too long nor too short—and
as slender as those of a deer. As I am praising the palfrey, I
should say that it had short pasterns and high feet, all equally
black, which were sleek and beautiful whether or not a groom
curried it.

[7366] It was so perfectly formed that a man wise enough to
know the nature of all creatures could not imagine anything
better if he sat thinking about it for eight whole years and
reflected on nothing else but what a beautiful and faultless
palfrey should be like. This would be the result. If he then had
the power to give substance to his ideal, just as he pictured it,
and could place it before him and take away whatever was not
pleasing, it was so perfect that he would not remove a single
hair. Should someone say, "He is lying," I'll explain the matter
so that he will understand that the account is true.

[7393] The palfrey was not native to the country, and I'll tell you how it came there. Once when their host had ridden into the forest looking for adventure, as was his custom, he took it away from a wild dwarf as it stood in front of a cave. Having tied it fast to a branch, the dwarf had gone off, and the king discovered it there and untied it. When the owner returned and didn't find it by the tree, he was greatly distressed. Seeing it then in the hands of a stranger, he began to cry and wail loudly and witness to the merit of the palfrey by raging with grief. He wanted to give three thousand marks of gold if he could keep it, but the king, not needing the other's wealth, refused every offer and led the palfrey away. In his misery the dwarf now raised such a clamor that the mountain resounded. The saddle on it was worth more than its weight in gold. However, to keep the story from getting too long, I'll say only that it was too small for a full-grown man.

[7433] The king brought the palfrey out of the forest to Penefrec and gave it to those for whom he had taken it, his two sisters. He thus showed his fondness for them, because it bore one gently and swiftly: I'll tell you how. It put its feet down so lightly that no one, no matter how keen his senses, could ever hear them. And truly, the one who rode the palfrey felt as if he were floating on air. If it were not excessive and improper to speak so much of a palfrey, I could tell wondrous things about it. But I shall not do so and shall praise it no further. At any rate—they may say what they will, relate many stories, and give their opinions—no man ever had such a fine palfrey. Why should I say more?

[7462] On the palfrey was placed a lady's saddle which, as we have been told, displayed a great deal of expert work. The most skillful saddler who ever lived, a craftsman called Umbriez, labored on it for a long time, devoting all his attention to it for three and a half years, until he completed it according to his plan. To tell you just how this saddle was made would be too hard for a simple fellow like me, and even if I could do it justice, this would take a single tongue too long. I am also hindered by not having seen it myself. However, as briefly as possible I'll let you know something of its workmanship according to the account of him from whom I got the story when I read it in his book.

[7493] "Now wait, my dear Hartmann, and see if I can guess."
All right. Be quick.

"First I must think about it."
Hurry. I haven't time to waste.
"Don't you think I'm a wise man?"
Of course. For God's sake speak up.
"I want to tell this . . ."
Only about the saddle. Nothing more.
"It was made of hornbeam . . ."
Yes, what else?
"coated with gleaming gold . . ."
I wonder who could have told you?
"very firmly put together . . ."
You heard rightly.
"and covered with a fine wool cloth."
I have to laugh at this.
"You see how well I can guess."
Yes. You must be a good weatherman.
"You talk as if you were making fun of me."
Oh no! As God is my witness.
"But your mouth looks amused."
I'm always ready for a laugh.
"Did I really guess it then?"
Yes. You really don't know what you are speaking of today.
"Then I wasn't right?"
By no means.
"Are you saying that I lied?"
[7523] No. Your untrained fancy simply betrayed you. Let me tell you about it. Consider the size of a grain of sand. There wasn't that much wood in the saddle. It was of ivory, precious stones, and the best gold ever refined in the fire, with no impurities. The master made it from these materials with great skill: he arranged the ivory and jewels in a pleasing manner, as elegance dictated, and used gold inlays to hold it all together.

[7545] The saddle was engraved with the long poem of Troy. On one side in the front was the account of the events connected with its conquest and destruction. On the other side it told how the wise Aeneas sailed away over the sea to Carthage, where the mighty Dido showed him her favor, and how he then did not keep his promise to the lady, but deceived and forsook her. One side of the rear saddlebow was engraved with the story of her great sorrow and of how she sent messengers to him but failed to change his mind. There was a clear account of his noteworthy deeds from that time up to his conquest of Laurentum: to tell of the way Aeneas seized it would take too long. The other side gave the tale of his marriage to Lady Lavina and of his rule there, which continued without misfortune until his death.

[7582] Covering the saddle was a fine silk and gold cloth of the best workmanship, which hung down low, almost to the ground. On it could be seen all the world's wonders, one after the other, that the sky encloses. If you don't mind, I'll name some of them to you, although I'll have to leave out many more. The four elements were there, gleaming in their special colors, and by each stood those things subject to it, all portrayed with great skill. The first of the four, the earth, appeared with its beasts—tame and wild, of field and forest, more than anyone could know—and also the human creature, which was wrought with such mastery that it seemed about to speak and be more than a mere image.

[7610] Nearby surged the sea, in which was a lifelike fish together with all the sea monsters and other beings that live on the sea bottom. If someone gave me their names, I would be glad to learn them and pass them on to you. Look for a man who can tell you what they are, and if you don't find one—which can easily happen—take my advice and set out at once for the sea. You will find a host of creatures in it. Go stand at the shore and ask them to come out to you onto the sand: then you will get to know them. If that doesn't work—which also is possible—go down to the depths yourself, where you will get to know them to your great sorrow and little profit. So I would counsel my friends not to be curious but to stay here at home. Whatever can readily harm a man at any time without doing him any good, comrades, is not worth bothering with.

[7642] The third element was there too. Do you want to know what this is: the air with all its family. In it many kinds of birds hovered, woven with such art that they seemed really alive and flying up into the sky. Fire also appeared on the cloth, with its dragons and other things that live from fire. The cover ended with a border, the breadth of a hand and embroidered with jewels, that almost touched the ground. It was indeed a splendid cloth that bore Jupiter and the goddess Juno when they sat on the bridal throne in their lofty realm, but it could compare with this saddle cover—I assure you—only as the moon with the sun. You must admit that I am telling you the truth.

[7669] The stirrups were costly and beautiful. They were broad gold rings which were shaped like two dragons. The goldsmith's hand that devoted itself zealously to them knew well how to make them—the tails arched around to the mouths, the wings were spread as if for flight, the eyes were jewels: four fine jacinths. Of what were the girth and stirrup straps made? You would have to look closely to tell whether it was silk trimmed with gold or gold lined with silk. Indeed, you would not know that it was a fabric without feeling it. From the appearance alone you would never guess. The buckles were strong and splendid, made of silver so that one could see a white gleam in front of the gold.

[7694] The saddlecloth was elegant. It was not a calfskin, like many I have seen—one couldn't find a bit of leather there—but was artful and lovely. It went well with the saddle and was of like quality. The cloth was carefully stuffed and soft as cotton, and could not chafe the palfrey. The part which showed below the saddle was thickly quilted and was adorned with pictures showing how Piramus and Thisbe, overpowered and crazed by love, had a sad end when they came to the fountain. In place of a crupper, there was a net woven of strong gold threads which was spread over the rump of the palfrey. Many precious stones were set in the netting at the places where the threads crossed and the meshes were fastened. There was a ruby in a blue enamel setting at each knot, and these stones gleamed brightly about the palfrey's haunches.

[7730] The breaststrap was graceful and practical, both beautiful and strong. Like the reins, it was a ribbon two fingers wide, and into it the eleven precious stones were artfully woven. The twelfth was set alone at the front of the bridle in a broad disk that lay against the forehead and under the forelock. The shining carbuncle, which is always bright, served a purpose there in that one could see by it if one had to ride on a dark night. Between the eleven jewels which were spread along the breaststrap hung pretty little golden bells that one could hear from afar. The saddle was made of such things and better than I have described. Indeed, it seems to me fitting and proper that it should be much more beautiful all in all than any other, for truly it was given to the most beautiful lady then living, the noble Enite.

[7767] Their horses have now been brought up, and it is time for them to depart. Did they then say farewell to the court? Yes, to everyone, from the young people to the king's sisters. These two equaled any women who ever lived in their firm resolve to do good. They were the true guardians of good manners and had reached the point where they were named among the first whenever noble ladies were singled out. My Lady Filledamur and her sister Genteflur gladly did all that a woman can do to earn the love of God and mankind.

CHAPTER 5

The Joy of the Court

[7788] Enite then rode off with Erec and their host. The palfrey carried her along the road so gently that he whose ship moves safely with a favorable wind on a calm sea never travels with a bit more comfort. They intended to ride at once to Britain to King Arthur; however, they did not know yet at which of his castles they would find him. As they went along, King Guivreiz said, "We shall find him at Karidol or perhaps at Tintajol." They rode uncertainly and somewhat at random until noon, when their horses brought them to a crossroad on a pretty heath. Since they did not know which way led to Britain, they chose the more traveled road and thus missed the right one. Later, after having gone about five leagues, they saw a large and stately castle before them. Guivreiz was troubled at the sight and sorely regretted the chance that had brought them there.

[7826] "Now tell me, why?"

I know and shall say at the proper time, which has not yet come. How impatient you are! Who would want to get ahead of his story? Still I shall not refuse to tell what the castle looked like: listen to how the account goes.

According to the tale, it was an excellent site, twelve hides in area and on a round rock which, without any humps, was as smooth as if turned on a lathe, high enough to be beyond the range of catapults, and in every respect all one could desire. The mountain top was enclosed by a high, thick wall, and the castle within made a splendid sight. Above the battlements projected

120

towers made of large, squared stones which were not held together by mortar but were tied much more firmly by iron and
lead clasps that bound them tightly in threes. The space between the towers was filled with houses in which the castle
dwellers lived in splendor.

[7861] The stronghold spread out in a square, the towers of
which—thirty in all—were adorned above with red gold bosses
that shone far over the countryside. This showed the stranger
who chanced to be riding that way where he was, for he could see
the gleam at a great distance and could not miss the castle by
day. At the foot of the mountain a river dashed with a great roar
through a chasm so deep that it seemed to one looking down
from a seat on the battlement as if he were seeing into hell, and
dizziness would draw him toward the abyss with such strength
that he would flee to safety. On the other side, where the road
went up to the castle, stood a prosperous settlement with many
buildings, which extended in one direction to the river and in
the other to a lovely, wide park, as beautiful a one as has ever
been seen, so my source told me.

[7894] When Erec caught sight of the castle, he asked Guivreiz if he knew the place and what its name was. "I know it," was
the answer. "We have strayed far from the right road. God damn
it! As often as I have ridden this way, it has never happened
before. I have made a bad mistake and taken us off to the left.
Britain lies in that direction. Let's turn around while we still
have enough time, and I'll lead you back to our road."

[7911] "Noble lord," replied King Erec, "should we ride away
thus? Since we have come so close, come along for my sake in
order that I may take a look at the castle. I must see it. The
outside is so beautiful and imposing that I am sure there will be
many things inside worth viewing. There will be ladies, too. You
must allow me to get to know it."

"It will be too bad if you do, and I shall be very sorry if I have to
let you."

"What do you mean, King Guivreiz?"

"I mean only what I know."

"For God's sake, tell me."

"Just turn back. It will be better for us."

"I wonder why you say that."

"You will find out if you don't go back."

"I must learn what is there. At the worst it will only be death."

"You can easily get into such danger that your friends will never cease to mourn for you."

"For God's sake, will you tell me about it? I would like to know what it can be."

"Turn back, as a favor to me, and I shall be forever indebted to you."

[7943] "That wouldn't become me very well, because you might think that I gave up the undertaking through fear. Moreover, there is no terror which you couldn't at least tell me about. If it were of such a nature that I should let it be, I would do so."

"King," said Guivreiz, "I shall tell you as much as I know. The danger is great, but in hope that you will give up this visit, as you suggested you might, I shall let you hear what it is. This is Brandigan Castle, and many noble knights have ridden here boldly seeking adventure, but every single one has come to shame and grief thereby. Although it has been going on for a long time, nobody has succeeded, and all have suffered the same lamentable fate: they were slain. What more is there to say? I can only fall at your feet and implore you to take my advice and turn back. This adventure is such as to make my heart fear that you will come to the same end as the others who journeyed here."

[7982] "I would be a shameful coward," replied Erec, "were I to turn back without even learning the rest of the story. Can't you tell me what it is about or what it is called? I would always feel disgraced if I were afraid of something of which I knew nothing. Why have you so long avoided giving me a full account of the matter? For whatever happens to me, I truly will not leave without hearing more."

[7997] "I'll tell you just what the adventure amounts to," said King Guivreiz then, "because you insist. It is called *Joie de la curt.*" Since this word is unknown to Germans, I shall explain it. It means: joy of the court. "Do you see the park below the castle?" he continued. "For a long time a knight has lived there, and the reward of the adventure is simply that whoever undertakes it has the right to find out if he can defeat him in combat. The knight is the nephew of the lord of the castle, and it has always been clear that no one in the country compares with him in strength and courage. He has killed all the knights who have ridden against him to win the adventure: no one can withstand him. Do me a favor and don't go on."

[8028] Laughing loudly, King Erec then spurred his horse ahead. "Forward, noble knight," he said. "If it is only a man whom one must defeat, the case is by no means hopeless. Why did you make it sound like such a great matter? Is he a mountain or the like that one should fear him so? I thought that the castle must be full of dragons and fierce beasts that would kill us as soon as we came there, no matter how we defended ourselves. As it is, I expect to go on living even though, God willing, the knight shall not be spared another trial of his strength. If he kills me, then I'll be dead: that will be no great loss to the world." The noble King Guivreiz could easily see that Erec fully intended to go through with it and that no one could stop him. It was fear of this which had troubled him from the moment he first saw the castle. Indeed, no objections did any good—Erec was determined to ride on—so they set out on the way.

[8057] When King Erec with his lovely wife rode toward Brandigan to risk his life, there was much merriment in the town below the castle, with dancing and all sorts of games that young folks like. As they approached and the people caught sight of Enite riding in front of the two men, everyone said that he had never before seen a lady whose person and clothing, palfrey and riding equipment were so beautiful. Because of pity, their gaiety vanished at once, and all of them began to lament bitterly the charming lady and the fact that such a fine man should lose his life, which they did not doubt.

[8086] "Almighty God," they said, "why is it that you created so perfect a knight and did not show your full grace by keeping him from making this unhappy journey, for he will be killed here. Oh, you poor woman! How distressed you would be if you knew what will happen to you here. How sad will be your bright eyes, now joyous and carefree, and your red lips that make people smile at you. And how sorrowful your gay spirit will become when you lose your husband." All bewailed her fate: not loudly, but in a murmur in order that the knight could not understand them.

[8112] They said much more, and many women beat their breast, while others wept bitterly. The noble Erec knew why they did this, but acted as if he noticed nothing. He was undaunted and cheerful, as a brave man should be who cannot easily be upset by words. He was not superstitious and foresaw neither loss nor gain in the murmurs of the women, just as he paid no attention to his dreams. He also did not believe in weather omens, and it made no difference to him whether an owl or hawk flew across his path of a morning. Moreover, he never had a fire built of dry twigs so that his fortune could be told or made use of any other such art. He didn't care whether the lines in his hand were close or far apart and observed no superstition at all. He was so confident that, however the people tried to dishearten him, he took it as a joke, and it did not move his manly firmness a hair's breadth.

[8147]"As long as God protects me," Erec thought, "nothing can harm me. And if he doesn't want to grant me a respite, I might as well die now. Life has to end sometime." Light of heart, he rode up to them, greeted them with a smile, and began to sing a happy song. The people then muttered, "It seems that you don't know what is going to happen to you here. Soon, unfortunately, before this time tomorrow, your merry song will come to a sad end. If you and your wife knew how short your joyful life will be, you would stop singing."

[8170] The brave man thus came up to Brandigan, where he was received very well and in keeping with his station. Accompanied by his retinue, the lord of the castle came forth some distance from the gate to greet Erec, both glad and sorry to have him as a guest. He was very much afraid that the knight would lose his life; otherwise he was welcome. The lord showed this to all three, for they were treated with great respect.

[8187] It was still not late in the day, and when the noble guests were in the stronghold, the lord and his retainers amused them as well as they could with many stories so that they would not become bored. After a while he asked if they wanted to join

the ladies and, at their pleased assent, led them up a stairway
into a palace so beautiful—if my source does not lie—that the
goddess Pallas would have been satisfied with such ladies' quarters when she ruled on earth.

The room was round and splendidly adorned with fine marble
that pleased the eye and was as beautiful as one could wish.
These varicolored stones—yellow, green, brown, red, black,
white, and blue—were polished until they glistened like skillfully wrought glass.

[8221] The guests saw the loveliest women sitting there. Who
could describe and praise them to you as they deserve, for the
like of this beautiful group has never been seen. Eighty ladies
were there, who were dressed alike because all had put on fine
and costly mourning clothing. This and the fact that they never
laughed showed that their hearts were sad. Their dresses and
mantles were of black samite, but neither the sleeves nor the
sides were trimmed with lace. They were not inclined toward
pomp and pride at that time, so I have been told. Their hair was
artfully bound by white fillets which were quite ordinary and
simple and without gold adornment.

[8250] When the guests entered, these ladies received them
with more joy than they felt, as is often done by a sensible person
who avoids troubling another with his sorrow if he can. The lord
went to sit with them, as did also his guests: Erec, Enite, and
Guivreiz. As his eyes passed from one to another, Erec thought
the first lady beautiful and the next more so, but less lovely than
the third, who in turn was surpassed by the fourth. He granted
the prize to the fifth until he looked at the sixth, whose splendor
was dimmed by the seventh, who could not match the eighth. It
seemed to him that the ninth should wear the crown, but then it
appeared that God had devoted more care to forming the tenth.

[8273] The latter, however, was excelled by the eleventh, and
she by the twelfth. The thirteenth would have seemed perfect
had it not been for the fourteenth; the fifteenth lady was all one
could wish, but her beauty was nothing compared to that of the
sixteenth. Still, he preferred to look at the seventeenth lady
sitting there, and the eighteenth pleased him more than any
other until he saw the nineteenth. However, he liked the twen-

tieth lady best of all. Who could describe them? The beauty of the least charming of these women would grace an imperial throne.

[8292] Having carefully observed the delightful group, Erec thought to himself: "Mighty and gracious God, I can see that you are rightfully called the wondrous God, since your power and decree have gathered into so small a space enough beautiful women to adorn splendidly many great lands, as you know, which you now leave joyless." Thinking of this, he became silent.

[8307] Meanwhile, the host was telling the ladies why the stranger and his wife had come. When they heard this, the ladies were at once reminded of the sorrow which had befallen them all, and their faces—which just before had been cheerful and lovely—became pale, as tears drove the blood from their nose and cheeks. Erec did not know what it meant until Guivreiz told him. "Do you see the grief of these noble ladies?" he asked. "They were the wives of the knights who were slain here. Why couldn't I persuade you to give up this journey! The lovely Enite must stay here, too, if you do not win the combat."

[8334] Erec's heart was deeply moved by the ladies' distress and because they, who were created for joy, were spending their young lives grieving, for their faithfulness made their pain as great now as when it began. Now and then they looked at the stranger with troubled eyes, lamented his handsome figure, and were filled with pity that his wife, as they firmly believed, was to remain with them there. "May God forbid that I should let my wife be added to this sad company," thought Erec. It was a mournful sight for the guests, because they were distressed by the ladies' sorrow.

[8359] Since it was now time to go, their host led them to dinner. Nothing was overlooked: they were served a great plenty of all that belongs to a feast. They had finished eating and were sitting there speaking of all sorts of matters when the king of the land asked if they had encountered anything noteworthy along the way. After the guests had related to him whatever they knew that was of interest, Erec said, "My dear host, people far and near have told me many wondrous things about the splendor of this castle. I shall not ask concerning them because I have seen it myself and must agree that the reports are indeed true. However, I have also heard that one can have a contest here with a brave knight for a great prize and would like to know what it is all about. Tell me this, sir."

[8390] The king was silent for a while, sitting there with lowered head in deep sorrow. This was because he was an upright man, and his kindly nature was troubled by the stranger's question, for he had already learned that the knight had come to undertake the adventure. Distressed, he tried to think of some way to prevent this, some means—seemly to both of them—to change his mind and keep him from being killed. At last he looked at the knight and said, "Sir, I want to give you such good advice as I owe my guest, the most welcome one, moreover, whom I have ever had and one to whom I wish the best of fortune. Let the question drop and forget about this adventure. Last year and this year, in truth for twelve years altogether, much harm has come of it. Besides, we both have seen so many other things about which we can talk and thus pass the time. Let us speak of something else."

[8424] Erec answered him as a bold man whose heart was resolute and more steadfast than a diamond, of which one has said that if it were placed between two grinding mountains of steel, it would wear them to dust before it would show a single mark—what could be more wondrous? Yet this man's bravery was even more constant, for a certain type of blood will soften the diamond and nothing but death itself could conquer his spirit or make it cowardly. With a laugh Erec said, "Matters about which I dare not ask must be fearful indeed. However, I did not inquire because I am thinking of winning fame denied all those who have come here before me, but because I would be annoyed—if people should ask me about it—not to be able to say anything. Since I have been here, they would declare that I was lying."

[8458] The king believed him and related what I have already told you, just as Erec's companion had done on the road, only he told in full and explained better some things that Guivreiz had slighted. He said that the park was strongly protected and that no one who valued his life should try to enter, even though there was no wall around it. "In it," he continued, "lives with his lady a

knight so strong and valiant that he has killed all those whose
hearts could not be dissuaded from seeking adventure. I tell you
that any noble knight who comes here with this in mind needs
only to go to the park gate. It will open as soon as he speaks and
he can walk or ride in, but others must remain outside. The gate
then closes, and the matter must be settled by the two, for,
whatever happens, they will have no arbiter.

[8494] "I don't know how it will be from now on because no one
has come to him for more than six months, not since he killed
three men whose names I can give you. They were among the
best knights in the world: Venegus, who missed no chance to
show his courage; Opinaus, who never fled from anyone; and
Libaut of the land of the Wends, who had won great fame. When
these have lost their lives, there is no use in your trying. With
your leave, I'll give you the best advice, which is to refrain from
fighting him, for the mighty man is accustomed to cutting off the
head of the one he has defeated. If you do not believe it and want
to see for yourself, that will also be your fate."

[8520] "I knew that there was a road of Fortune somewhere in
the world," said King Erec, "but I didn't know just where. So I
rode forth at random to look and now have found it. God has
shown me his kindness in leading me here to a game after my
own heart, one in which I can risk little to gain much on a single
throw of the dice. I have sought until this day, and now, thank
God, I've discovered it, a chance to stake a penny against a
thousand pounds. How lucky I am to find such a game here. Let
me explain myself better. You have just told me that this lord is
perfect in knightly skill and courage. He is therefore very famous and is praised in all the lands for his great deeds. On the
other hand, I unfortunately have not performed such feats and
have little renown. Since I have done few of the things that
make a knight well known, I have remained obscure to this day.
I am therefore happy to risk my little repute here, to increase it
to great fame or lose it entirely.

[8560] "See how differently the same game pays us. If God
grants me the honor of defeating this knight, I shall become
highly esteemed, while he cannot win even a twelfth as much.
He will be putting his gold against something of no value,
because he will be little praised and have no glory for gaining

the victory over me since he has often done as much and I would soon be forgotten. I assure you that he won't be spared, but will have to fight me."

[8576] "Tell me, my lord," said Erec's host, "why should you be more dear to me than to yourself? But now it is time to go to bed. Should we live to see tomorrow, I'll take you to him if I can. Nevertheless, I advise you in good faith to think better of it. That would seem sensible to me, because I pity you if you enter the park—you will never see us again. You may be sure of it."

[8589] "As God wills, sir," replied Erec. Then they went to the bedrooms: one for Erec and Enite and another close by for Guivreiz. The rooms were well provided with costly bedding and other furnishings, and had many fine wall hangings that were painted with gold. The flagstones were covered with splendid carpets, which their host's riches could well provide and befitted his high position, for he was the ruler of the country, King Ivreins. He treated his three guests with great honor and ordered the servants to give them the zealous attention that mighty kings should have.

[8614] Erec and Enite yielded themselves to their love and lay happily together until morning. His heart was not entirely free of manly concern. Indeed, it is said that one who knows no fear is a fool, not an ideal man, for no heart was ever so bold but that justified fear well befitted it. Still, however readily one may dread that which threatens his life, one must have no cowardly fear, and there was none of this in Erec's heart.

[8632] Since he was to fight that day, he did as wise men do—because there was reason for concern—and got up very early to go with Enite to a mass of the Holy Spirit, where they both prayed earnestly that God would preserve his life. Erec was glad to take communion, as a knight is who has a valiant man to fight. After the mass he left the church. Meanwhile, breakfast was prepared, an ample meal which he hardly touched: three bites of chicken seemed to him enough. Then a drink was brought to him and he drank St. John's blessing. Thereupon the knight armed himself and got ready to ride into the park. Enite had never before been so distressed: the tears flowed from her eyes like rain.

[8660] The town was now full of the story. As you have already heard, all the people knew that a knight had come who intended to fight the one in the park. King Ivreins wanted to look on and his retinue wished to be with him, so the castle was emptied except for the sad ladies, who remained there. They had suffered such pain that they did not want to see anything which would add to their sorrows, the greatest of which was that death would not take them. The town's lanes and roofs were crowded with waiting people when Erec rode down the castle road toward the park. Above the low murmur of the throng he heard many disheartening comments, which predicted nothing better for him than certain death. They said so many things of this kind that he would have lost his courage then if forebodings of evil and reminders of his great danger could have daunted him. However, he took it as a joke and was not affected.

[8698] If our source book tells the truth, the park was so devised as to arouse the wonder of all of us, both wise and foolish. I tell you that there was neither a wall nor a moat around it, nor was it enclosed by hedge, fence, water, or anything tangible except a level trail, and yet a person could walk or ride into it only at a single, hidden place on one side, where a narrow path entered of which few knew. Whoever chanced to go in there discovered all sorts of delights to please him: many kinds of trees that bore fruit on one side and were filled with lovely blossoms on the other, beautiful songs of birds that made his heart rejoice, and sweet-smelling flowers of manifold colors that covered the earth until not a hand's breadth of it was bare.

[8730] The odor of the fruit and blooms, the contesting voices of the birds on every side, and the sight itself were all so charming that anybody who entered with a heavy heart would soon forget his troubles. One could eat as much of the fruit as one wished, but would have to leave the rest there, for none of it could be carried out. Perhaps you would like to hear what tightly enclosed the park, for I am sure that few people today know of the magic that did this. There was a cloud around it through which no one could pass except where I told you.

[8754] King Ivreins rode toward the park at the head of the company in order to show Erec the way to the knight and brought him, at his request, to the hidden entrance. Here everyone stopped except these two and Enite—and Guivreiz, who was also allowed to ride farther. Only the four, no others, went on and soon came to where they observed what they could rightly call an unusual sight. A large ring had been marked off by oak posts, and on top of each, to Erec's surprise, was a man's head. Only one was empty, and from it hung a large horn.

[8777] When Erec asked the meaning of this, his host said, "You should have stayed away, because you will deeply regret having come. Your desire for fame has misled you. Now you can see the truth for yourself and know that I did not lie. If you still doubt me, look at the heads that the knight cut off. And I'll tell you more: the empty post is waiting for you; it is to hold your head. However, should you or any other man escape this fate and defeat the knight—which is impossible, otherwise it would have happened long ago—then you or he should blow the horn loudly three times to announce the victory. This is why it is there. This man would gain lasting fame and be honored above all others throughout all the lands. But why talk about it, for it won't happen. I don't believe that he who is to blow the horn has been born yet, because the rest of the knights now living are nothing compared with the one here. Since you won't give up the attempt, noble knight, I pray that God may be your shield and have mercy on your soul: no one can save your life."

[8817] As soon as the beautiful lady saw the dreadful sight and heard these discouraging words, all pleasure and joy vanished from her heart, if indeed she had brought any with her. Her color and strength left her as she became deathly pale with grief and fainted: the bright day turned to night as she lost sight and hearing. This showed that, however many sorrows she had endured, she had never in her life suffered greater distress than now. Deeply concerned, her host and her husband tried to revive her. When she came to and looked up, Erec said bravely, "Don't worry, my sweet Enite, you are weeping too soon. Why are you so troubled? I am neither sick nor dead; indeed, I am standing here in the best of health.

[8845] "You should wait until you see me bleeding, or my shield chopped to pieces, or my helmet cut open and me dead. You will have time enough then to weep. But first there will be a battle to decide between us, and we can't be sure who will be the victor. I have been assured that God is still as merciful as ever,

and the man whom he wants to protect always comes through
unharmed. I am certain that I shall live if it is his will. Your
weeping pains me, and you wouldn't lament so bitterly if you
knew how I feel. I'll tell you the truth: were I to have no other
courage but that which you give me, I could never fail. The
thought of you makes my hand victorious, for your love gives me
such strength that nothing could prevail against me in a long
day of conflict."

[8874] Erec now had to part from his companions—who were
very worried about him—and ride on. The lord of the castle
showed him a narrow, grassy path which went beyond the posts,
and Erec followed it alone, leaving the others behind. I don't
know what will happen to him. No knight was ever more uneasy
than he as he rode this fearful way which filled his comrades
with gloom. May God's power protect him now and save his life!
Let us all join his wife in prayer that God will grant him the
victory.

[8896] For about three times the length of a charge King Erec
rode along the grassy path through the park, surrounded by
flowers and bird song. He then saw before him a beautiful and
splendid tent which was large and tall and made of two kinds of
samite in black and white strips that were skillfully painted.
Portrayed there in pictures of gold were men and women, birds
that seemed to be really flying, and all kinds of animals with
their names above them. In place of the knob there was a finely
wrought eagle, inlaid with gold. The tent ropes were round, of
silk, and of many colors: red, green, white, yellow, and brown.
This tent which was set up on the grass displayed both pomp and
comfort. Sitting under it was the most beautiful woman Erec
had ever seen—except for Enite, who was more lovely, it must be
admitted, than any other woman of that time or this; she was the
child of Perfection, who had overlooked nothing which could add
to her beauty.

[8937] The lady who sat there was splendidly dressed in a
costly samite blouse, which gleamed like brown glass and was
elegantly trimmed at the wrists with sable, and a long ermine
mantle. Her hair was bound with a ribbon. What was her skirt
like? You will have to ask her chamberlain, for God knows I
never saw it: I have seldom been in her presence. Erec couldn't

see it either because the mantle was wrapped closely about her. The sumptuous couch on which she rested had a large frame of silver and was of fine workmanship.

[8958] When he caught sight of her, Erec courteously dismounted and tied his horse to the branch of a tree. He leaned his shield and spear against the trunk, removed his helmet, and wedged it on the rim of the shield. He then took off his cap, for he was very well mannered, and approached the lady. She would have preferred that he had stayed away, because she was afraid of being annoyed, but she greeted the knight since custom required it.

[8973] The lady received him with these words: "Sir, I would give you a friendly welcome, but one should not be deceitful in a greeting. If it were not that you must suffer injury and disgrace here, I would have been glad to see you. Who advised you to come? Or were you moved by the desire of your own heart? If so, you have in your breast a disloyal counselor whose treachery will cost you your life. Leave me, sir, for God's sake, because it will mean your death if my lord catches sight of you, and he is nearby."

[8990] Even before she had finished warning him, he heard a loud, fierce voice that sounded like a horn, so large was the throat from which it came. It was her husband. In full armor, like Erec, he had left her in order to take a ride through the park and look for something to do. Then he saw the stranger standing in front of the lady, thought this foolish and disdainful, and turned to hurry back to him. Erec saw him while he was still far off. The lord of the park was large and tall, almost a giant in size, and was roaring threats. His mighty horse, his shield, his surcoat, and his armor—so I have heard—were all the color that suited him: fiery red. I think he must have been distressed whenever he found no one to fight, he was so bloodthirsty.

[9024] The lord now rode up to the intruder and addressed him in a harsh and angry voice. "Tell me, you scoundrel," he said, "who told you to go so close to the lady?"

"What is wrong with that?"

"It is very foolish."

"Sir, of what are you accusing me?"

"I think you are too bold toward the lady."

"Your words, sir, are immoderate."
"Say, who brought you here?"
"Good friends."
"Well tell me, who?"
"My heart and my will."
"They gave you poor advice."
"They have guided me well thus far."
"That will end here."
"It need not."
"Why are you in armor?"
"Sir, the armor is after all my own."
"Do you want to fight me?"
"If that is what you wish, yes."
"Stupid fool, what are you thinking of?"
"You will see."
"The conflict will turn out badly for you."
"You should say: 'God willing.' "
"How dare you take my words so lightly?"

[9049] "I care nothing for your threats. They remind me of the two great mountains that swore by their wits that they would get themselves a handsome child, one as large as they. Then God ordained it to become a laughingstock, and they brought forth a field mouse. Mighty castles have burned down from small fires, and those who act so fierce sometimes lack courage: this will be seen here. Before we part today the boasting will end for one or both of us."

[9067] "I can promise you that," the red knight assured him. At these words Erec hurried back to his horse, tied on his helmet, quickly got everything else ready, and mounted. The other also did not neglect to prepare himself. Then both braced their shields firmly, spurred their horses forward in true fury, and galloped boldly at each other as fast as they could go. Their thighs moved up and down as if they were flying. The ashen spears were then lowered and pointed at the four nails opposite the handgrip of the shields. The aim was good, and each struck his target as his spear passed through the shield to the mailed hand, but no further. In spite of the powerful thrusts, the strong shafts were not broken, so they pulled them back and eagerly rode away from one another with the same intention: to joust again. Once more the horses were roughly spurred and driven at each other.

[9106] There was born here an ardent passion with a great prize. They made love without a bed, and the goal of their passion was the death which would come to the vanquished. They kissed each other with the spears that passed through the shields with such amorous fervor that the shafts splintered right up to their hands and the chips flew like dust. Under the weight of the knights, the horses collided with a force which drove them back on their haunches and stunned their riders, who dropped the reins and sprang off. Lord God, deign now to watch over King Erec, for he is facing a warrior whose courage and strength make me fearful of the outcome.

[9134] The knights drew their swords, swung them back, and, stepping up to one another, brought them down on the shields. These were held before them to catch the fierce blows, but were soon cut away down to the boss so that there was not even enough left to protect the arm. Useless, they were thrown aside, leaving the knights with only their armor to protect them from death. The swords threw showers of hot sparks when they landed. So many furious blows fell that one must wonder how the swords and helmets survived. The very large man often drove the smaller one quickly back for some distance, but then Erec would force him back just as far. They struggled this way and that until the grass and flowers were all crushed and it was no more green underfoot than if it had been midwinter. The battle continued thus from morning till noon.

[9169] "Tell me, friend Hartmann, how could they keep that up?"

They got the power from their ladies. The one who was sitting there affected her husband in this manner: if he began to despair, he needed only to look at her, and her beauty gave him new vigor so that he regained his strength and fought boldly like one who had rested. He could therefore not be daunted. I'll tell you also about Erec: whenever he thought of Enite, her love strengthened his heart and sharpened his wits until he too fought with new might and manly courage.

[9188] After this had gone on for some time without either being injured, the large man thought: "It enrages me that this little fellow has withstood me so long." He gripped his sword angrily with the intention of felling his opponent and took a big swing. The devil knew no pity, and his heart gave his arms great strength as he brought it down with a will on the middle of Erec's helmet. He struck the knight so hard that the blow produced a broad flame which would have set fire to a bundle of straw. (May God reward him who believes this, because I can't swear to it.) The fearful blow resounded in Erec's head until he almost fell. Since both eyes and ears failed him, he could neither see nor hear, and it would have been the end of him if the sword had not broken. However, he quickly recovered and could see, hear, and think as well as before. He was troubled by the pain, but more by shame that anyone should get such an advantage over him, and he now took revenge on the one whose skill and power had made him so weak.

[9230] Gaining strength from the thought of his beautiful wife, Erec retaliated for his mishap by taking his sword fiercely in both hands and trying to wound the other by flailing away at his hard steel armor. The red knight, although he seemed like a mountain compared to Erec, had to retreat from the blows since he had no weapon. This was no disgrace, because I know for certain and as well as I know anything that he would have fought back and not taken the blows without returning them if his sword had not broken. As it was, Erec drove him backward with powerful strokes and quickly avenged the mighty buffet he had gotten. He did not strike as he had done before, but savagely and wrecklessly. With blows landing one after the other and one beside the other, he beat on the knight's armor until his sword began to glow and the quality of its edge quickly worsened. Its brown color faded, and it broke as the other had done.

[9263] Well, what do you think Erec should do? He threw the piece left in his hand so hard against the chest of his retreating adversary that the knight almost stumbled and fell to the ground. However, the devil kept his footing and saw that the sword was broken and Erec's hand was empty.

"I'll get vengeance now," thought the red knight and sprang fiercely at Erec. He intended to seize him quickly, lift him high in the air, and crush him by dashing him to the ground with all his great strength. Fortunately, among other useful things that

Erec had learned as a boy—in England, as I've heard—was to wrestle very well. He also had the advantage that it is hard to hold onto a man in armor. The large man, therefore, could not carry out his plan, for Erec slipped out of his grasp, grabbed him by the belt, and kept the lower part of his own body back to prevent the other from pulling him close.

[9296] Erec then showed his strength. When his opponent bent over him, he braced his shoulder against the knight's chest so that the latter could not get at him, pushed him violently away, and then jerked him back with such quickness that he lost his balance. Because he was heavy, the large man could not recover, and fell to the ground. At this the surprising Erec dropped down on him with all his weight, knelt on his chest, and beat him with mailed fists until the prostrate man could endure it no longer and ceased to resist. In despair he asked his smaller opponent for a truce. "Knight," he said, "let me live a short time and then take my life."

"Do you admit your defeat?"

"Not yet."

"What do you want then?"

"Noble knight, stop a moment and tell me who you are."

[9327] "You have never seen that happen," replied the one on top, "and you won't now. It would be strange indeed if the victor had to surrender to the vanquished. If you want to live a while, take some good advice and tell me quickly who you are, where you came from, and whatever else I may want to know."

"You are mistaken if you think I will," said the red knight. "Even though you have beaten me and are holding me down, I choose to be killed unless you will tell me your name and station. Should this defeat have come at the hands of a commoner or someone who never before won a battle, I would rather die than yield. If, however, God has granted that your birth makes you worthy of it, then be so kind as to stop fighting, since I shall be glad to yield and satisfy all your demands. I beg you in God's name to be truthful, because, should you not be a nobleman, my life will end here in any case, for I shall be disgraced. It would trouble me much less to die honorably than to live dishonored."

[9366] "I shall gladly do your will in this matter," answered the noble Erec with a smile. "Even though it is not customary,

I'll tell you: my father is the mighty king of Destrigales, my mother is of like birth, and my name is Erec."

"Can I depend on that?"

"Yes, indeed."

"Then let me live and accept my oath of allegiance. See, I am at your disposal and offer my service, which you would lose if you should kill me. I'll give you my name: it is Mabonagrin." Erec was merciful and granted him his life.

[9387] After the knight had yielded, Erec helped him up and they untied each other's armor—there was no one else to aid them—and took off their helmets. Their enmity vanished and they wished one another honor and well-being, as friends should. Then they sat down together on the grass, because the struggle had left both of them very tired.

[9401] They now talked for some time about all sorts of matters having to do with their separate concerns as well as with that which they had undergone together. Finally King Erec said, "I have heard that the lord of the castle here, the king of Brandigan, is your uncle. Indeed, I have learned a little about all your affairs, and your situation is clear to me. Yet there is one thing I don't know: tell me, having been in here so long, how do you pass the time with no other people around? Although it is delightful here and although nothing makes the heart so light as when two lovers like you and your wife are together, still one really should withdraw from women at times.

[9425] "I have heard them secretly admit that they are not offended when their husbands come and go. Even though they won't confess it openly, they like to have a man seem new to them and not be with them constantly. Moreover, it would be better for this lady, who has spent all these years in here, to be with other women. I am really surprised that such a handsome knight as you could remain here, for it is very nice to be with other people. Were you ordered to or do you hope that God will reward you for it? Are you supposed to stay forever?"

[9443] "I'll tell you the whole story," replied Mabonagrin. "I didn't choose this life of my own free will, for no one ever more enjoyed being among people than I do. Now listen to the strange circumstance that caused me to begin this life. I had to do so or break my word, and but for God's help, which in mercy he has now given, I would have grown old here. Today it ends, through a mishap, to be sure, yet one which I can easily get over.

[9459] "Sir, I'll tell you to whom I made the promise. Once in my youth I rode off to another land, where I met the lady here in the care of her mother. She was only eleven, of a noble family, and it seemed to me that I have never seen a more beautiful child, girl or boy. When I first caught sight of her, so lovely and noble, I took her into my heart, for I was no older than she. I began to court her at once, with such success that she ran away with me. As soon as I brought her home to this castle, my uncle decided to wait no longer, but to dub me a knight at once.

[9486] "The rites were performed in here. Afterwards my lady and I were sitting at the table and were in the middle of a meal when she obtained an oath from me in this indirect way. 'My dear lord,' she said, 'remember what I have done for you,' and asked for a favor in return. She urged me strongly and bade me make a solemn promise to do whatever she might request. My love for her forced me to promise—to be sure, I had no idea that she would want anything that I wouldn't be glad to do. However, I would have granted her whatever she desired that was honorable and in my power, and I still do all she asks: I am sure that she feels the same way toward me.

[9508] "Her wish is my desire, and whatever I want she gives me. How could the bond between man and wife be full of love if they are good friends only physically, while their minds are so divided that one craves something, great or small, that the other does not? There is no such discord between us. In a hundred years I would not waver a hair's breadth from the belief that my true happiness lies in doing her will, for most of my joy consists in carrying out her wishes in every way I can. She is equally devoted to me. I therefore would harm myself much more than her if I did not gladly do whatever she asked.

[9532] "When I gave my word, she embraced me with joy and said, 'How lucky I am, for God has granted me such a delightful gift to enjoy: I hold in my arms everything my heart desires. Fate has been kind to me, and I'll presume to claim that the park in which we are sitting, which I would praise above all others, is a second garden of Eden. See the splendid display of many-colored flowers and all kinds of birds. How lovely it would be to

live in here! This is where I want to enjoy your love. The gift I
ask of you is one which will ensure that I remain yours and have
no need to be afraid of other women. It is that you stay in the
park with me, just the two of us together, until the time that a
single knight defeats you—here before me, so I can see it with
my own eyes and be certain.'

[9562] "Now why did she do that? I shall explain it to you: she
thought I was such a fine knight and had no idea that it would
ever happen that anyone could be found who could defeat me.
Indeed, no one ever did until today, as I can easily prove if you
doubt it. Do you see the heads? I cut all of them off myself. And
I'll tell you more: the post over there without a head, where the
horn is hanging, was waiting for the next knight. I had you in
mind for this one and expected to put your head on it. However,
God has preserved us both from that. I feel that I have gained
from my defeat, since you have set me free. God sent you here.
Today my troubles are over: I'll go out and travel wherever I
wish.

[9590] "I'll tell you something more. Your coming was truly a
great blessing for this court, because it lost all its merriment
with me and was stripped of its pleasures. There have been no
festivals of any kind since I left—because, for all my youth and
noble birth, I was buried alive—and the *Joie de la curt* entirely
disappeared. But now they shall begin them again, because they
have their favorite back. Your brave arm has freed this troubled
land from great sorrow and led it back to happiness. You will
always be honored for that.

[9610] "Sir, get up now and go joyfully to blow the horn. It is
there so that if someone should defeat me, he can at once let
people know by blowing it three times. It has hung there un-
sounded during the long period, much too long for me, that this
has been my home." He then took the horn from the post and
asked Erec to blow it. He quickly put it to his lips and sounded a
great blast, for the horn was large and long.

[9628] When the sound of the horn was heard, the people
outside the park who were awaiting the result of the conflict all
looked at each other in surprise, because no one had any idea
that the knight Mabonagrin would be defeated. They thought it
an illusion until Erec proclaimed his victory with a second and

then a third blast. Breaking the old custom, King Ivreins of Brandigan, who alone knew where the entrance was, at once led Enite into the park. With joyous clamor, the entire throng then hurried to where Erec and Mabonagrin were, greeted them cordially, and celebrated the occasion by singing happy battle songs.

[9661] After having long been sad at heart, they were now gay, and they honored Erec with high acclaim. All cried with one voice: "Knight, we praise you! May fortune never forsake you whom God sent into this land to help us. We extol you and wish you joy, flower of all knighthood! God and your brave arm have won you the crown of glory over all lands for all time. May you live long and happily!" They showed their delight in many ways.

[9680] The beautiful Enite was also not sad at this time. I will swear that the moods of the two ladies—the one who gained most from the conflict and the one sitting under the tent—were not the same: neither spoke, but the heart of one was singing. She was as happy as she could be, while the other wrung her hands at her husband's defeat and was filled with grief because she and Mabonagrin were no longer to remain in the park. When Enite saw her sitting there weeping, she showed a womanly heart, as her kindness caused her to greet the lady despite the latter's pain. Then they talked back and forth for a while about joy and sorrow and thus became friends, as women do. They asked about each other's family and homeland and, losing their reserve, told all they knew. The two soon found out that they were related and indeed quite closely, for Enite's uncle, Duke Imain of Tulmein, was the brother of the lady's father. They also learned, so I have read, that they were born in the same town, Lut.

[9725] See how sorrow vanished then: they were so pleased to find each other that they embraced and wept with joy. The tears soon gave way to laughter, which was more fitting, and the ladies went hand in hand to their husbands. They were so happy to learn of their kinship that they couldn't wait to tell everyone about it. All who heard the news maintained that it was providence which brought them together in a foreign land.

[9744] The people now left the park. The heads which had

been cut off there, as you have heard, were taken down from the posts, and messengers were sent throughout the land to bring priests to give them an honorable burial. May God reward Erec for this! The festive mood at Brandigan grew rapidly, and for a good reason. As soon as the report spread over the land that the lost joy of the court had been restored, all the king's vassals and relatives set out for the castle with their ladies in order to see what the new merriment was like. The nobility gathered here. The king and all the guests that he could by any means induce to come celebrated a festival that lasted with feasts and entertainment for four weeks. The dreary life he endured because of his nephew ends in gaiety as a wealth of pleasure makes up for his former sadness.

[9779] Since the king would not let them go sooner, the three companions remained for the celebration, but Erec was not happy; indeed, his heart was sorely troubled. Being a compassionate man, he was grieved whenever he thought about a certain matter, and the eyes of such a person often fill with tears—whether he is alone or not—on seeing that which arouses his pity. This was so pitiful that no one capable of compassion, however happy he might be, could have refrained from weeping at the sight of such distress: I am sure of it. Erec was sorry for the wretched company of eighty ladies who, as their sad demeanor showed, were bereft of all joy. Those whose husbands had been slain by the red Mabonagrin spent the days weeping and lamenting. Like the hunted hare who does not stop to graze, they fled in grief from any place where they might hear the sounds of merriment. Moreover, as long as they lived they would never willingly have looked at the man who had caused their suffering.

[9816] It was apparent that Erec shared their sorrow, because he soothed their pain somewhat with kind words of comfort and he and Enite never left them if it could be avoided. What helps one more than being consoled after some great misfortune? One friend owes this to another.

Erec counseled them to remain no longer, but to improve their lives by taking leave of the king and coming with him to King Arthur, since they could not be happy here in this castle. They gladly took his advice and asked for permission to depart. Their host readily granted it, for he had been told that they had said they could never have any pleasure at Brandigan, so bitter was the pain they had suffered there. He didn't mind letting them go if they could change their lives for the better, but if they could have been content at his court, he would not have wanted them to live otherwise than in his care. The king willingly outfitted them for the journey. In keeping with their wishes, he supplied them with mourning clothes and with suitable mounts so that the colors of both apparel and horses were alike and harmonious: a somber black.

[9858] When the festival was over, Erec departed, taking the ladies with him. This was a kindness, because they could never feel at home there. The lord of Brandigan mounted a beautiful Castilian and his retainers their fast horses, the best they had, and escorted the company a long distance. At last Erec asked them to come no farther, gave them his best wishes, and rode on with the ladies, whom he brought to Arthur's castle. He was most welcome here. All those at the court noticed at once that the women were dressed and mounted alike and they maintained with good reason that they had never seen such an unusual group, so many ladies wearing the same color. The ones who did not know what was behind it kept asking until Erec told them the story.

[9888] The entire retinue then rewarded the noble knight for his troubles with the crown of honor: it was said in his praise that no one in the world matched him for bravery, because none in all the lands had succeeded in such great adventures. Even he could not have done it if Dame Fortune had not helped the wet nurse care for him while he was in the cradle. While the members of the court looked at the ladies with wonder, the noble queen led them to comfortable quarters. She was glad to treat them most kindly without being asked. May heaven repay her!

[9910] King Arthur was happy to have these guests in his castle. After he had waited a while, he thought the time had come to go to them, which pleased Erec, Guivreiz, Gawein, and all his knights. "Lords," the king said to them, "let us go and greet the ladies who have just arrived and console them in their sorrow." Then he and Erec got up and quickly led the way into the women's quarters, which held more ladies than ever before.

Their host and his companions sat down with them, some here, some there.

[9932] When the king saw how they suffered under their misfortune with like laments, pain, steadfastness, loyalty, beauty, youth, modesty, good manners, kindness, disposition, spirit, and clothing, he thought it womanly and good. His heart was moved and he was pleased. "Erec, my dear kinsman," he spoke up before them all, "you deserve to be praised and honored constantly, because you have greatly increased the splendor of our court. May he never again be happy who does not wish you well."

"Amen," they all responded, because they desired only good for him. The sorrowing ladies were prevailed upon to honor the king by turning their hearts and lives to joy, and they let him exchange their mourning clothes for dresses of silk and gold which were more suited for pleasure.

[9963] Erec, the darling of Dame Fame, and Guivreiz the Small were received with all the respect befitting their station and zealously feted until the news came to Erec that his father was dead. For the sake of his country, it was now necessary for him to give up his wandering life and return home: the people and the land needed him. He therefore took leave of King Arthur in order to journey to his own castle. When he left the court, he gave as much as he could to the poor, who could use his wealth, each according to his need—even if they did not beg—so that all sincerely blessed the knight, praying that God might guard his honor and be merciful to his soul. King Guivreiz rode away with him in order to return to his own realm, and the two were given an imposing escort to the place where their ways separated. Here they parted—with no enmity, I am sure, but as the best of friends—as Guivreiz went toward Ireland and Erec toward Karnant.

[10002] Erec's subjects knew both the day and the hour when he was to enter the country, and six thousand or more of the noblest of them were chosen at once to honor him. Since they were anxious to see him, they rode hurriedly toward Erec for three days to welcome him, and no one can truthfully maintain that he has ever seen a warmer reception. Impelled by the loyalty they owed him, all greeted their king with courtly rejoic-

ing and gaily decked horses. Those who were knights and could afford them held splendid banners which matched the caparisons and were richly adorned with strange figures. The field was colored red, white, yellow, and green by their silk clothing, the finest in the world.

[10032] The people of Karnant in the land of Destrigales thus received their returning lord into his kingdom in a manner befitting a mighty monarch. According to a reliable report, he had succeeded in winning such fame in many lands that no one then living was as highly praised for brave deeds. Because of his renown, he was called Erec the Wonder-worker. He was present near and far, in all the lands. You ask how that could be? It was this way: when his person was in one place, his fame was in another, so that the world was filled with him. None other received like acclaim.

[10054] When God had sent him home, to the joy of his country, Erec arranged for a festival that was more splendid and attended by greater lords than any ever held in that land before or since. Many of his peers came, whose names I would be glad to tell you if I knew them. Here he received in glory the crown which his father, King Lac, had worn before him with honor, for he too had done many bold deeds. Never was an esteemed sire better replaced by his son. Who could be more suited to follow him? May God bless Erec's reign, since he is the rightful heir. We must also wish him well because he began it well, with festive hospitality. For six weeks a mighty throng of knights and ladies could be seen there, and whatever one wanted for his pleasure throughout that time could be found in abundance.

[10083] Erec ruled the land so that it was at peace and did as the wise do who thank God for whatever honor they win and regard it as a gift from him. Many are misled by a belief which indeed deceives them when they become proud—that everything good they receive comes to them only through their own merit—and they do not thank God for it. Then such benefits can easily end. However, King Erec did not behave thus, but praised God at all times for exalting him. He therefore had everything his heart desired, for the lord of heaven preserved his honor from all stain until his death.

[10107] Lady Enite had endured hard times in foreign lands,

but she made good use of them. Now they came to an end and were replaced by comfort, honor, and manifold splendor. She too had all she wanted for the rest of her life, because, to her great joy, God had sent her father and mother to live in her land. The king took care to fulfill her desires wherever he could, but his devotion was governed by propriety and not as it was formerly when he became indolent because of her. For he lived as honor demanded and in such a way that God, rewarding as a father, at last gave him and his wife eternal life in exchange for an earthly crown. Pray, all of you, for God's sake that the same reward, which makes us his vassals and is worth more than gold, may be ours after this life of exile. Here ends the story.